THE SUMMER OF THE ELDER TREE

THE
SUMMER
OF THE
ELDER
TREE

Marie Chaix

Translated by Harry Mathews

DALKEY ARCHIVE PRESS
CHAMPAIGN / LONDON / DUBLIN

Originally published as *L'été du sureau* by Éditions du Seuil, Paris, 2005.

First edition, 2013

Library of Congress Cataloging-in-Publication Data

Chaix, Marie, 1942-
[Été du sureau. English]
The summer of the elder tree / Marie Chaix ; Translated from the French by
Harry Mathews. -- First Edition.
pages cm
"Originally published as L'été du sureau by Éditions du Seuil,
Paris, 2005."
ISBN 978-1-56478-852-8 (pbk. : alk. paper)
1. Chaix, Marie, 1942- 2. Authors, French--20th century--Biography. I. Title.
PQ2663.H259Z4613 2005
843'.914--dc23
[B]
2013003456

Cet ouvrage a bénéficié du soutien des Programmes d'aide à la publication de
l'Institut français/ministère français des affaires étrangères et européennes

This work was supported by the Publications Assistance Programs of the French
Institute / French Ministry of Foreign and European Affairs

Partially funded by a grant from the Illinois Arts Council,
a state agency

www.dalkeyarchive.com
Cover: design and composition by Mikhail Iliatov
Printed on permanent/durable acid-free paper

for Richard Morgiève

One day something happened to me. One day I lost confidence and decided not to write any more.

There are stories you can tell people three times, six times, people who are friends, who are close to you, even very close. They barely remember them or, as they listen, recognize their importance so little that they forget them. A year or two later they repeat the same question.

The fact is, they are all taken up in their own stories and don't listen to other people's. Or they listen and then forget. It's normal enough after all.

In March 2013, thirteen years had passed since this story occurred. Not a day goes by without my thinking of it. Aware that it was blocking my way, I often tried to write it down. It resisted, like a curled-up cat weighing on my sleep. I waited. I told the story less and less.

How do you explain to people who've read my work (often all my work, one book leading to the next) why "it" has stopped? After writing and publishing eight books, why was I no longer capable of finishing one other? How confess that I'd lost the thread of my integrity?

Sometimes I had the feeling I understood everything. At other times I was in total darkness. Between the two something crucial for me must be hovering, something I could write.

Alain Oulman's death backed me against a wall and left me
stranded there. Inside me an unfamiliar woman responded: I
won't write anymore.

It was he I wanted: as editor, as friend. It was *his* approval I
wanted. For him I might have accepted the exertion of a literary career, to please *him*. I had the means to do it; I knew it was
what he wished. Forsaking my potential talents like this would
disappoint him. But he had abandoned me, and I decided that
he was irreplaceable.

He would tell me, Write! and I'd write. I'd send him my
assignment. He would say: could be better. I'd grumble and
redo it. Better. Or else he'd say one word, nonchalantly indulging in a hint of commentary that would open up a new path, a
whole horizon. I'd start over again.

He asked questions; he listened, his eyes shining silently,
with the silence of love, with a loving smile, a generous expectation that I could not possibly disappoint.

I wrote for him; because he loved me so that I'd write. It was
for me that he existed. It never occurred to me that he might
exist for others. His gift to me was: he existed for me.

He died. After that, nothing. Words lost. Without him, no
faith in words. Nothing but this wall, a plane of opaque glass
where I was left suspended. Punished in front of the class for
a mistake I hadn't made, mortified with resentment, watching
the others romping in the schoolyard, writing their books for
fun, the lucky souls. How I envied them!

Alain was sixty when, without warning, he died. To me—ha-
bitually on my guard—his disappearance was a total surprise. I
was devastated. I had never thought this man might be in dan-
ger. When someone has saved you, you cannot imagine that he
might be weaker and closer to death than you.

He had taken me in when I was lying at the edge of a ditch

(it was more like an abyss). I found no pleasure in anything—I'd just been thrown out of Le Seuil, shown the door of my own publishing house, bye-bye and thank you very much. No, not even thanks.

"I'll publish you. We've got work to do," is what he said after reading my stillborn manuscript, which I didn't know how or where to bury. Here I was with Alain Oulman, editorial director of the Calmann-Lévy publishing house, acting like a madwoman, lost, Alain bending over me, his voice filled with great tenderness, saying, "Marie, I'll publish you, but in my opinion Le Seuil won't let you go."

People who write will understand me: manuscripts are children whom we present at the temple, sick with fear. If the child is rejected, it's not a tragedy, it's a funeral. You get over it. Maybe.

Le Seuil let me go. Nothing could be simpler: I only had to ask, in writing. I swallowed my shame rather bravely, I think. Anyway, the hell with it, Alain and I were deliriously happy: we were free.

"And now start writing!" I was duty-bound to him, and drunk with gratitude.

The novel was to be called *Le Fils de Marthe*. It's about Jean, a young man who dies in an accident, and a year in the life of his mother, who mourns him, emerges from her grief, and starts living again. One of the reasons given by Le Seuil's selection committee for refusing the book was: Marie Chaix can only write autobiography. She didn't experience this story firsthand. QED.

Under Alain's wing, I went over it from start to finish. For four months we worked together in a complicity of elation and tears, spending hours in the office on Rue Auber seated in our uncomfortable and beloved red-velvet armchairs. Conspirators in melodrama and its literary uses, we'd float on a tide of emotion and gaiety: moments of creative joy that recalled the intense ones spent with Barbara when, leaning on her piano, I listened to her composing her gloomiest songs. People never laugh so much together as when they're in despair.

Sometimes, when it was his day at the office, another of Calmann-Lévy's editors (since deceased) would stick his head through the door—Roger Vrigny, who had given me so much encouragement in his droll and solemn manner—and say complainingly, "Alain! I've got to talk to you. Make her do her writing at home!" He'd swagger off, a cigarette between his lips and a pile of manuscripts in his arms.

The book came out at end of January, 1990.

March 29 of the same year: I'm alone in our Paris apartment. Harry is in New York. No one has called all morning. In its two months in the stores the book hasn't caused a storm; in fact there's not a breath of wind. Alain phones almost every morning: "Don't let it discourage you. The reviewers are a little scared by the story of the kid's death. Marie, don't worry about a thing. I'm confident."

It's a little after eleven. The phone rings. It must be Alain. The voice is that of Jean-Étienne Cohen-Séat, the CEO of the publishing house. In astonishment I hear: "Marie, I've got bad news. Alain didn't wake up this morning." Oh? thinks the spellbound idiot, what business is it of Jean-Étienne's if Alain wants to sleep late? . . . Those irretrievable seconds when everything falls apart . . . Hang up! I'm alone, with a knife sunk between my eyes.

I won't write any more

For ten years—and by dint of repeating the fact it's now a good eleven years — I "haven't written." That intrigues me.

Obviously this doesn't mean that I haven't written "at all"—several dozen notebooks are stacked in that "at all"—but there's no disputing, even if I dip into them here and there for "odds and ends" to soothe my anxiety, that I haven't written anything that is presentable or fully accomplished or that, simply, satisfies me. So this still adds up to "nothing"; and that intrigues me.

Being so stubborn. Building myself a rampart out of this magma of manuscripts. Being so bad tempered. Being constantly on the lookout for the slightest paranoid justification, something (given the state of mind I indulge in) I invariably end up finding.

For instance: *Le Monde* of January 28, 2000, in which I noticed an article by Pierre Deshusses on Jacques Le Rider's book, *Journaux intimes*. Let me quote a few excerpts that reveal my propensities as a furious stalker of lethal statements.

This is how the article begins:

"Whether as an out-of-the-way fragment or real material belonging to one's œuvre, the temptation of the private diary affects almost every writer. Often thought of as the recourse of those incapable of serious work . . ."

Of course the next subject that came up was dear old Amiel, who "in almost 17,000 pages compiled over a period of thirty years, devoted himself to self-analysis, finally reaching the disillusioned conclusion that a private diary is 'an excuse for laziness, a semblance of intellectual activity'; the slow perishing of a subtle mind (adds Monsieur Deshusses) that is incapable of extricating itself from that narcissistic temptation whose only issue is death by drowning."

I was already gasping for breath. Was it possible that I'd become the dear old female Amiel of my time? Then came the final blow, in a reference to Goethe and his "negative judgment of the private diary":

"Even Kafka"—even Kafka!—"whose diary remains one of the richest and most indispensable, suffered from this Goethean conception of the form that has perpetually created a sense of insufficiency, always reminding the writer as he writes his diary that he is incapable of genuine writing, of keeping a distance from his anxious, suffering, tormented self."

So what's left? Stop reading? Stop writing? Really stop?

While these fruitless ruminations kept me stagnating, an unexpected event burst in on me as if in answer to the questions I glumly kept asking; it both unsettled my moroseness and overwhelmed me.

The Facts

On April 14 of the year 2000 my daughter came back to Paris from America and told her husband she no longer wanted to live with him.

With their three-and-a-half-year old son, she had just spent Easter vacation at our place in Key West. From her fitful, allusive confessions I was well aware that a storm was on its way. I never thought that it was so close at hand and so destructive, or that she would be so determined.

The day before I'd driven them, mother and child, to the Key West airport, where they'd barely caught the plane to Miami. We parted in a hurry. With his little knapsack of odds-and-ends bouncing on his slender shoulders, César waved his hand in my direction. We didn't even have time to kiss each other good-bye. I loathe departures.

Before they'd been caught up in the rush, with the sound of propellers filling the warm air, Émilie shouted to me in the dramatic, petulant tone of a little girl angry that I'd refused her a fabulous present, "Can't you understand I'd just as soon have missed the plane?"

What would that have changed? She's made up her mind.

Soon afterward, I was back in the lovely wooden house they'd just abandoned, enclosed in tropical greenery, a narrow paradise of orchids and trickling silence. Holding a bundle of dirty laundry tight in my arms, I sat on the ground in tears. Images dimming, sounds diminishing: a little boy capering over the boards of the deck, echoes of his laughter against my cheek . . .

With this departure something had been shattered, suddenly and irremediably.

Images Dimming

It's strange all the same. My daughter leaves her husband and I'm the one who feels abandoned, as if it were I who'd lost him. Their separation has broken my heart. What's happening to me? Why today has their story become mine? And where are these tears greeting their breakup coming from? From what depths, where old heartaches sleep?

What kind of suffering is this? What face does it wear, and by what right has it through me taken over their nine years of private life, as if it knew their secret, and left me to watch the distance growing between them, unable to restrain them, like a boat left adrift in the current?

The feeling that it's him I've lost: and underneath these words, what lurking darkness is hiding, ready to devour me?

What have I been so afraid of during all the time that writing has escaped me or that I've turned my back on it?

Richard

A month later, on May 15, 2000, I met Richard at a café near the Odéon in Paris: a lanky man with large black eyes (his son's are the same). He said, "When I saw her arrive at Charles-de-Gaulle, walking toward me with our son in tow, I knew. I saw it was all over."

He added point-blank, before I could even get over the emotion of seeing him, "Start writing! You have your subject. Write, get in touch with what's most secret in you. Be daring. Don't let the pain wear off. Get started."

"Don't make me laugh," I answered, blowing my nose.

It wasn't the first time he'd hit the bull's-eye with me in the ten years we'd known each other.

This tall, jovial man (then forty-one) first came into my life on March 18, 1991, carrying a bottle of champagne. Émilie had phoned me: "Please meet him. Have lunch together. Tell me what you think . . ." I don't see what I might have told her—everything seemed to have been settled and set on its irreversible way.

They'd met in the office of his publisher, where she was working as an intern. At the age of twenty-two she was giving up her inconsolable first lover. And he, for her sake, was leaving everything—wife, house, and two daughters, the youngest aged nine.

She had fallen violently in love with Richard, she told me, when she read *Un petit homme de dos*, the book about his father. She then went on to give him my first book, *Les Lauriers du lac de Constance*, about *my* father.

This exchange of books—trying to make a connection through the intimacy of words and a conflation of families—

had left me flabbergasted. In a letter in which he spoke of my book and how it had touched him, he added, "Madame, the day when your daughter's eyes met mine, I'd have done better if I'd broken both legs."

And here he is at my door with his bottle of champagne. I take an instant liking to him—his laugh, his beautiful hands popping the cork. We drink out of my grandfather's Baccarat champagne glasses. He recognizes them and says, "In his glory days my father had wineglasses with the same pattern. I've still got two or three of them."

There's no need for me to say much: he never stops talking. Straight to the point. One of his first pronouncements: "You ought to write about yourself."

I burst out laughing. "That's all I ever do."

"I don't know everything you've written. What I've read seems to me to be a memorial of love for your family."

"True enough—a memorial for the dead."

"Well, you're alive. You're my sister, don't dawdle. Start writing!"

Write?

May 26, 2000

At the Haut du Peuil, facing a closed window on a gray afternoon in a gray May, I'm counting flies. I feel like a dunce. My eyes wander toward the hill, far off, beyond the fields and highway; a landscape checkered by the cross of the window frame that divides the poplar beyond the garden into four squares of greenery.

With a few exceptions, writing has always been tedious for me. Sometimes it's as if I were back at school—elementary school, the school for beginners, when you had to force yourself to get your composition done. You couldn't think of anything. "How did you spend your vacation?" The sense of tedium was awful.

If I move slightly to the right, I perceive the poplar in only two of the four panes, but not the elder tree underneath the window. Its bushy growth, brutally cut back by Harry last fall, as yet gives no sign of the shape it will take this summer.

In the garden of Upper Suresnes where I spent my childhood, there was an elder tree that must have been many years old. A thick trunk, worthy of the name, cut off at about four feet, provided a kind of launching pad for tall, flourishing branches sturdy enough to climb in.

This unusual elder was my refuge, the first tree I'd ever known, loved, and watched through all its astonishing changes.

The foliage of the elder tree isn't very elegant, but it's profuse. Its matte-green, pointed leaves are rather ordinary; it's their abundance that forms the lovely masses that make it look like a fluffed-up head of hair.

The shrub is rarely slowed down by any pruning inflicted on

it: it heads right back toward the sky, putting out shoots that are at once stiff and soft. The wood of its branches is singular. When young, it's covered by thin gray bark that a penknife easily peels off to reveal a second skin, delicate green and soft as watered silk. And what a joy it is to dig out of its sheathe the dense, squeezable marrow lodged inside each branch! But the glory of the elder lies in its flowers, broad, creamy-white umbels that abruptly grace these undistinguished bushes with the solemn atmosphere of Corpus Christi, of young girls dressed for their first communion swarming over the landscape . . .

The garden of Suresnes is vast, dense, full of dark hidden places that can't be reached by the voices of grown-ups, those strange creatures saddled with their own boring concerns.

So as not to hear them whispering, shouting, and complaining, I used to escape into the trees and sulk.

Born (by chance, no doubt) of parents considered "old" at the time—they were both in their forties—I was the last of four children. Anne, my sister, was eight years older than I, my brother Paul thirteen. As for the oldest, Jean, he was no longer around. We spoke of him only in our prayers.

In those first postwar years, our household still included my mother, who used to leave early in the morning and come back at night worn out; as well as Juliette, my omnipresent second mother, the one who kept our family running.

Our father wasn't there. All I knew about him was "what you mustn't mention to just anybody": he was in the jail at Fresnes, with the status of "political prisoner."

Whenever I heard my mother mention his imminent return (it took a good while to happen), I asked myself anxiously where we could squeeze him into our minuscule ground-floor apartment. It had been generously lent to us by my Uncle Pierre and Aunt Mathilde (my mother's sister), who had taken us in under disastrous circumstances in '44. They themselves lived with their two children on the third floor of this gray, austere cube of a house. My cousin Annie, an artist and a beauty just starting to flower, had been born the same year as my brother Jean, which meant she was eighteen years older than Serge, her little brother: another late product of chance, I imagine, and a lucky one for me—we formed a pair of inseparable rascals, as necessary to one another as Mutt to Jeff or Tom to Jerry.

The second floor of the gray house was made up of two apartments rented by two families. Juliette was on the best of terms with them.

That made for a lot of people at 2 Rue de Bellevue, a buzzing hive in the midst of a garden where—obviously without my suspecting it—writing put down its roots.

Every so often I was told, "What you've written isn't bad at all," or "You really should write . . ." Each time I was surprised and encouraged.

There was, for instance, a day during my first year at Lycée La Fontaine, in ninth grade. (By then we'd left Suresnes; our family had more or less regrouped in an apartment in the 16th Arrondissement.) The serious, portly lady with coal-black frizzy hair who teaches us French and Latin is handing back our assignments and criticizing our compositions, sometimes harshly, quoting our stupidities back to us. I'm dying of fright, worried about my grade, fearful of sarcasm and ridicule. The pile of assignments is shrinking. With her navy-blue woolen breasts resting on her desk, Madame Gaillard announces in slightly affected tones, "I'm now going to read you the best composition." The subject was "The song of the wind, the song of the rain." My heart beating, I recognize my own words. I don't know what to do with myself. I feel I'm going to faint with pleasure . . .

Writing a pleasure? Not often. The pleasure of having written: certainly. Another recollection from my lycée days: our philosophy teacher, Madame Davin-Roussel, is a comical, charming old lady with a mustache and a great enthusiasm for Piaget, the creator of genetic epistemology. Thanks to her, I was hopeless at philosophy (I would have been in any case), but I began writing short pieces that weren't too bad, if I can trust the pleasure she took reading them to the class when she returned our assignments.

"Mademoiselle Beugras"—that, alas, was my name*— "you've provided us with yet another of your little stories . . ."

One doesn't earn one's diploma with stories. I owed my *bac* to the "indulgence of the examiners," the dear woman having flooded my grade book with stupendous comments and acknowledgments.

It was another ten years before I started writing, but I've often thought that it was due to the blind generosity of this woman that I first derived confidence from words. She had put me on to something.

---

* See page 26.

What's happening to me?

"It happens all the time . . ." writes a friend in California to whom I must have sent a somewhat despairing letter about what was "happening to me." *"Why are you so upset?"*

She isn't the only one who finds my reaction exaggerated, given "what happens all the time," meaning couples who tear themselves apart and oblige their divorced children to keep running from one home to the other.

Fine. So instead of moping, why not try to understand the reasons for my confusion? It's amazing how many reasons you can find afterward, once it's over and love has evaporated, stranding two exhausted castaways who wonder what it was that kept them together, long ago. Do you remember?

Oddly, when I pestered my daughter with all the questions out of women's magazines that I heard myself uttering ("But why, why? What happened, when you loved him so much?"), the reasons she gave for her disenchantment were without exception the same as those that had excited her love, so strong, so immoderate, so . . . so . . .

"It's a difficult moment to get over," a friend briefly appearing in my summer tells me, "it's no fun seeing your daughter suffering." She hasn't understood anything, *I'm* the one who's suffering! "The funny thing is that it's *you* who are putting yourself in this state. You should keep things in perspective. After all, you did the same thing."

And I hear myself say, actually shout, "For God's sake! You've really got a nerve. That has nothing to do with it. Things don't just repeat themselves, they go back a lot further than that, way back . . ."

"Well then, take a look. Don't hesitate—start writing!"

Her too!

The woman who's provoking me today, on a horrible rainy mid-July afternoon in the Vercors, where I've had my fill of playing grandmother to my divorced little boy, no matter how much I adore him—the woman who's berating me in our Lans kitchen, a favorite place for indulging in confessions and fits of melancholy, is Nicole. It's funny. "Start writing." The same Nicole who one evening in 1964 at the Rosebud on Rue Delambre in Montparnasse, while we were drinking our whiskies (in her case a whisky sour, since she loathed the taste of Scotch) and smoking our Camels (ah, how pretty we looked in 1964!), the same Nicole who asked me irritably:

"Come on, just who was your father?" (He'd died shortly before; I was twenty-one years old.)

Answering in a stammer: "He was a collaborator. The prison at Fresnes. Uh, does the name Doriot ring a bell?" I clammed up, unable to go on.

"You're nuts. It's not possible. You've got to find out more."

Nicole: my Jewish friend, appalled by my political reclusion, staggered that in 1964 I knew *nothing* of my father's collaborationist past and was incapable of "telling what he'd done"; Nicole the very one who ordered me to "Write that story."

I'd obeyed. I'd written the story a very long time ago; I thought I was through with that part of my past. It's odd how wounds reopen in parts of you where you thought they'd healed.

A Young Man: Jean

During the fall of 1987 I was working on *Marthe*. It still had no title and I simply called it "the novel." I was with my daughters in Lans-en-Vercors in sullen November weather. One evening in front of the fire they asked me what I was writing. I told them a little about it. They were puzzled. "Haven't you anything more cheerful on offer?" Léo, then thirteen, wanted to know the names of the characters. "As a matter of fact," I said, "Martha, the mother's name, came to me all by itself. I don't know what to call the son."

"You're really dumb," Léo said to me. "Obviously he's called Jean."

Jean, my brother, the eldest of the four of us, died in Germany in 1945 at the age of eighteen. He'd had time to spend six months at Mainau, an island in Lake Constance, in the company of our collaborationist father. He had taken refuge there along with other members of the PPF, Jacques Doriot's shattered party.

To escape Paris and foreseeable retribution, my father had bade us farewell in the middle of a summer night in 1944. At the last moment, against the wishes of our weeping mother, he took his eldest son with him. He was put onto a truck loaded with part of the PPF archives.

My brother Jean adored his father. He used to say he'd follow him into the jaws of hell. Which he did.

In February, 1945 he was killed in Ulm by Allied bombs, no doubt on a train he was taking, in any case in the Ulm station: that's what probably happened. In the space of three days the bombing had left thousands dead in the town, among them a great number of whose remains could not be identified—the "missing."

In the immense green meadow of the Ulm cemetery, rows of identical white crosses stretch away out of eyesight, many of them inscribed where a name should be with the legend *unbe-kannt*: unknown. I say "many" because I stopped counting after the first few hundred, on a lovely summer day in 1963. I accompanied my mother who hobbled along, dragging her fifty-eight-year-old hemiplegic body down the avenues of that beautiful cemetery. So that she might accept, eighteen years after his death, that he was never coming back.

To her, Jean's disappearance was no proof of his death, and for eighteen years she had refused to accept it. I suppose that seeing so many of the missing aligned under hundreds of yards of lawn was reassuring: at least he wasn't alone.

Until then she had been secretly waiting for him. Miracles do happen. Sometimes amnesiacs have been known to reemerge. I knew what she was thinking about whenever she jumped at the first ring of the doorbell. Was the young ghost finally going to leave us in peace?

I was a two-and-a-half-year-old baby when the family fell apart that summer night. I can thus reasonably assert that I never knew my eldest brother. However, I was given no chance of ignoring him. To create indelible childhood memories I was shown photographs of him at every age; and all the women's sobs and whispers that filtered through the doors when they thought I was asleep had to do with him alone. I'd heard all about his difficult birth that had nearly cost his mother her life, his childhood anorexia, his green eyes that seemed to "fill up his whole face," his gift for languages and music. He was exceptional—the sweetest, the most ready to help. The best are the first to go . . .

No, no, my beloved, not gone, not really, he's still here with us. He's our protector. Better yet: he was your godfather, now he's your guardian angel. He's watching over you, he's at your side, just speak to him and he'll hear you.

My bedtime prayers were addressed to him, the serious young man looking older than his years in the framed photograph over my childhood bed. I was scared silly of hearing his voice dropping from the ceiling or feeling the fluttering of his wings in my ear. But the fairy tale seemed to make my mother happy. As for me, I didn't need an angel, what I wanted was my brother. So my only "real" memory of Jean is that of an absence, more burdensome than any corpse.

Of the three remaining children, I was the youngest, the one I think who suffered least from losing our brother. Paul, wracked by grief, concocted a fatal condition of high blood pressure that spared him till the age of thirty-three and no more. Shut into an adolescence of redemptive prayer, my sister, Anne, luckily found an outlet in music and words and escaped with minimal damage. So one can say that the Beugras girls came out of it better than the boys.

Beugras, alas . . .

That was my family name. In French it signifies, "I'm proud to be from Burgundy." (He was.) Or "I want my children to be proud of their name." (He said as much.)

My poor father—how we let him down! My two brothers by dying young; my sister, Anne, when she infuriated you by choosing a pseudonym for her singing career (the absurdity of your name for a performing artist never entered your mind); and I by grabbing the first husband who came along.

Beu/gras: *bœufs gras*, or "fat oxen." The name itself isn't easily borne, although things were worse than that. Obviously the *vaches maigres* ("skinny cows," meaning lean times) that echoed around the schoolyard at recess didn't enchant me. The pain lay elsewhere; and I didn't know it.

One incident during my adolescence could have put me on the right track. It only made me more confused.

Back to my school: I was paralyzed with timidity when I found myself in a vast Parisian lycée after years spent under the wing of Dominican nuns at the Pius X School in Saint-Cloud. There I am at thirteen, standing in terror on the classroom platform in front of Madame Poupard, our brilliant, irascible history teacher. She is quizzing me for the first time.

She looks me up and down with her prying eyes and scornful mouth. Her close-shaven neck makes her look like a bulldog. "Beu . . . gras." She repeats the name once or twice, cruelly emphasizing the first syllable, then:

"I've heard that name somewhere before . . ."

I don't flinch, hypnotized by an insinuation I'm unable to grasp. She studies my assignment book at length. Then, apparently relaxing, she starts asking me questions while still perusing me, he chin resting in her cupped palm. Overcoming my fright and jitteriness, I manage to answer. She nods her head, gives me a decent grade, and hands me back my assignment book without further comment.

It's with pity that I recall that lycée student, badly dressed, weighed down by her womanhood, constantly alarmed by a present she cannot interpret with words from the past—that unspoken past and its innumerable events of which she hasn't the faintest notion. Only scraps of stories have reached her ears, with nothing to make them cohere. No one has ever told her anything. So what does this Poupard want from her with her mysterious allusions to the name that she bears, that she drags around like some chronic pain, even if she's less obsessed by it than by the pimples blossoming around her lips or the stomach aches that torment her for a week each month?

"Beu . . . gras." The disgrace of such names sticks to us. A name is a burden. One in fact "bears" it and bears with it; it weighs on our life, when it doesn't threaten death—but that was a possibility I was incapable of considering barely ten years after the war's end.

Beugras, our father's name, was a depository of shame: a shame that oozed from the type on the front pages of newspapers at a time when I didn't know how to read; the viscous shame of prison bars when I wondered what he was doing behind them. Today I tell myself that it must be terrible to be the child of somebody one is ashamed of without knowing why, loving him all the same, without knowing why. Except that he is the father.

In my first book I took care not to give this father the name of Albert Beugras, preferring Albert B., transforming him into a character of fiction. Whom was I sparing? Him? No one remembered him except for a few surviving comrades in arms. When he left prison he'd been discretion itself. The family?

There was no male heir left, the sole fact that might have mattered to him when he spoke of "pride."

During all the years when I no longer bore my father's name, I never reflected on my concern with it. It's come back to me as something obvious: the woman who in 1974 signed her first book with her married name while revealing the scandalous career of Albert B., the collaborationist, hadn't yet expunged the shame of the adolescent girl standing terrified on the schoolroom platform under the eyes of her classmates and her *history* teacher. She was still her father's daughter, trembling (while hardly admitting it) at the idea of rejection, of being stigmatized by the book she'd dared produce.

Poor father, who at your trial for treason were still uttering that ridiculous statement about pride in one's name, with a haughtiness that almost cost you your life! The treason that you paid for, no doubt, but that settled lastingly on our heads like a crown of ashes no longer frightens me or makes me ashamed. It's all yours. I want no more part of it.

Grabbing the first husband . . .

It's only a quip, not wholly true but a little bit true all the same,
one that deserves a brief chronological comment if only to do
justice to the young man I fell in love with in April, 1968, and
who was to father my two daughters.

In '68, at twenty-six, I'm still working as Barbara's secretary.
I meet Jean-François in Paris on my return from my singer's
winter concert tour, which has come to a triumphant conclusion in Brussels at the little Théâtre 147, where she's given several performances. In the cramped wings where I scurry around
taking care of lighting cues and the continuity of the show,
a handsome, long-haired youth is casually manipulating the
levers of the console. We're the same age; we become friends.
"I'll call you in Paris," Christian tells me, "and introduce you
to my brother."

No sooner said than done; and well done.

The notorious month of May is approaching. Exhausted,
Barbara has to withdraw from the world and enter a clinic in
Garches for an obligatory rest cure. She will experience nothing
of May '68 other than the breathless reports I rush off to give
her in her waking intervals. We settle on a bench in the clinic
park, with horse chestnuts and birdsong overhead, and there I
unfold a tale of demonstrations, tear gas, flying cobblestones,
chants of CRS* = SS!

I won't go on about May '68, since I don't feel like a veteran
at heart—in fact I never was one, happy though I was to be
participating in those overwhelming events; curious, too; and
above all lucky to see them close up. Between the streets and
visits to Garches, I spent most of my time in the offices of Jean

---

* *Compagnie républicaine de sécurité*—the riot police.

Daniel's *Nouvel Observateur* where my friend Nicole had been working for three years alongside Guy Dumur.

There were to be two climaxes to my brief experience as a "68er." The first was the big demo where the slogan "We're all German Jews" was invented and where, submerged in the crowd on Boulevard Saint-Michel, shouting myself hoarse, I knew I was finally burying my collaborationist father; burying him a little deeper on Boulevard Montparnasse when I raised my fist and, not believing my daring, started singing the bits of the *Internationale* I'd just learned.

Second climax: the day of General de Gaulle's speech, when Nicole and I—two panicky innocents—found ourselves in the front ranks of a demo that had gone wrong, a few yards from the activists tearing up the street and the grenade launchers of the CRS, gray waves ready to engulf us. I had the fright of my life, and I never took to the streets again. My mother was very pleased about that. Immobilized in her wheelchair, she used to wait for me at home biting her handkerchief and finally stammering out, "You're not turning political, are you—like your father?"

She was hopelessly confused, and her daughter was in love, something that must have alarmed her as much as May '68, which for me in any case ended in a hospital where I was taken for an emergency operation.

Barbara had come home sooner than planned, unable to do without television, where she could watch the (dismal) sequel of events. And then, as everyone knows, there was gas again at the filling stations and the French went off on holiday.

Jean-François and I tied the knot a year later, on June 10, 1969—and that's what I wanted to get at with my statement: in truth my husband didn't "come along," it was I who provoked the marriage. A sudden obsession, at variance with all our post-May '68 principles.

The fiancée is six months pregnant. She's twenty-seven years old, her husband-to-be twenty-three.

In my circle, which includes family, friends, and my divinity, Barbara, no one approves of this abruptly concocted union.

Being pregnant makes the life of an artist impossible for me, but Barbara is generously waiting for the birth of the child before arranging our separation. As for my mother, physically weakened but totally alert, she can't understand. She can only consider the pregnancy an accident. We don't talk about it. A sensitive woman who has always loved her children passionately, she holds her tongue and keeps knitting while waiting for my time to come. But why marry? Or, in that case, why not a "real" wedding? No way, Maman! The young betrothed would see nothing in it but a crude imposture: he had fatalistically and somewhat cynically accepted the challenge, thinking he was yielding to a whim when in fact his name was being purloined.

Today, trying to understand such a conventional decision on my part, I suspect that I had more intimately buried motives.

As a child, I spent my vacations on the property of my grandfather, Louis Beugras, in Champagne-sur-Seine, the ugliest place to be found between Fontainebleau and Moret-sur-Loing. For me it was a friendly countryside, especially after we'd got past the gloomy black iron gates that protected my grandfather's domain. One walk that I was often allowed to take by myself led from the house to Saint-Mammès, a village on the banks of the Loing, to attend Mass.

I loved walking the mile and a half, leaving the road from Champagne and following the course of the river as far as the iron latticework of the old bridge that straddled it, at last reaching the square of this ever-so-pretty village of bargemen and the old church with its creaky, straight-backed wooden pews.

After Mass—my only memory of it is one of insipid bore-dom, but I endured it dutifully for my family's salvation and my own—I'd go to the sacristy to have the priest sign my cat-echism notebook, thus certifying my dominical regularity.

The way home was pure delight. My soul buoyant from hav-ing been a good little girl, purified by the communion wafer, I climbed the slope above the bridge and cut across the road to a hillock where I could gaze down at the motionless barges along the embankment, the steeple, and the squat houses.

I never met the wolf while skipping through the wild grass, but I did imagine myself in another tale: once upon a time . . . I'd cross paths with Prince Charming, he'd ask for my hand, and we'd be married in the fairy-tale church of Saint-Mam-mès. Deeply moved and of course beautiful in my spotless lace, I would mount the church steps on my father's arm, and he would proudly hand me over to the care of Prince Charming.

Are these traditional images, dreams of budding young girls, so innately engraved in us that they drape us, in a guile-less tremor, with the blurred outline of a white dress, with the expectation of a magical, timeless moment, with longing for a first time that will necessarily miscarry?

The pregnant young woman of 1969 has been fatherless for six years; she harbors no more fantasies of churches or bridal trains. The thought of getting married emerged from the depths of a night when, woken up by the joyous commotion of her child, everything around her exuded peacefulness. That moment of utter plenitude was abruptly dissipated by an irrational fear so deep and painful that finding a remedy for it became urgent.

Marriage is the most absurd proof of love that she can demand of the man sleeping peacefully at her side; but she knows no other way to soothe her fear—the fear of being abandoned, the primordial fear of being left without a man.

Her fear cries out in her, Make yourself one with the man whom you decreed to be the father of your child, don't let him run away, grant him the power to protect you, even if he doesn't want such a power; and he doesn't want it, and so what?

In the ornate wedding salon of the Boulogne-Billancourt town hall, I'm sporting my beige linen dress from Chez Victoire. I have no recollection of a bouquet. No one else is there besides our two witnesses, an actor friend of Jean-François's and my girlfriend, Noémie, in despair.

Was it to make up for the terribly conventional nature of a wedding that we invited no one? Simply getting married a year after May '68 was ridiculous enough—were we as well going to enjoy ourselves by giving a party? What nincompoops we were!

Our disappointed parents were informed the previous day. "Hardly time enough to send you flowers!" is what Jean-François's mother in Aix-en-Provence will say. "Flowers are the last thing we want!" As for my own poor, beloved, invalid mother, who would have dreamed of having grand organ music for her last-born little one, having been denied the town hall, she was allowed to provide the wedding lunch, served by a silent and reproachful Juliette.

Thinking back on that day fills me with nostalgia. It's like looking around at a landscape in which all the stages of dissension are already indicated. That very afternoon the first of them is waiting for us in the park of Saint-Cloud. "Do something, whatever it is—go out for a walk," my mother must have said, no longer able to cope with the situation. "Even if the sun doesn't join the party," Juliette mockingly adds.

The sky is gray. It soon may rain. All that remains for me

of these moments as hazy and flat as a faded photograph is the damp scent of box hedges, a sad, childhood, Palm Sunday smell, and well-groomed parks where boredom reigns.

The taciturn young husband paces along the paths as if alone in the world, a cigarette in the corner of his full, pretty mouth. He must be thinking, "What have I done?" Today I can understand him: the woman he has just negligently married is no casual Christmas present. She's four years older than he, the wild love she bears him is already hampering him, and then there is the child she so fervently wanted from him . . .

Whenever I come across photographs of the actor he was struggling to become at the time, what disconcerts me more than his young star's handsomeness is that he looks like an inconsolable child. I so wanted him to tell me, "I love you." He couldn't do it. And I wasn't able to console him. Did we come out even?

When I imagine the two of them in that gray June of '69, side by side in the wedding photograph that was never taken, I see they don't look like a couple; and I think, all the same, that they were right to try.

The child wanted from him

I learned of my first pregnancy in June, 1968, at the same time I was told that I had to be operated on the following morning: my unexpected condition had every chance of being cut short.

To this day I'm astonished by the reaction I then had. The memory of it is still vivid. Under the flabbergasted, disapproving gaze of the nun who was about to take a blood sample in preparation for the operation, I began dancing for joy. What had inspired this deranged twenty-six-year-old with such unbounded happiness at learning she was pregnant with a child that she would surely lose?

Only now, confronted with this theme of separation that seems to have guided my life, do I begin to understand that mother-to-be a little better.

Sometime in the 1980s I wrote this sentence in my diary: "If I hadn't had children I would have turned nasty." Rereading it I'm tempted to add "and gone insane." What do I know about that? Of something one has written, what truth survives?

I had, I still have a number of women friends who didn't want to have children, or were unable or no longer able to. They haven't inevitably "gone insane" or turned nasty. At least, not all of them. At that distant time when motherhood meant fulfillment, I couldn't understand these women without either children or the desire to give birth. They were foreign to me, they intimidated me, I didn't trust them. Later I became more tolerant, and I realize how for their part they must have mistrusted the mother hen I seemed to incarnate.

"If I'd hadn't had children" would I have dried up and withered in despair? Or, eroded by sterility, come apart like the rusty link that sunders the chain?

At the Clinique Violet, in June, 1968, the chain came very

close to breaking and reducing me to a little pile of rust ready to be claimed by nastiness.

The operation, a rarity for someone my age, should logically have left me gutted like a fowl ready for roasting if I hadn't fallen into the hands of a conjuror who salvaged the faint hope of another possible pregnancy. "Only if you are very careful," he gruffly added. Thanks be rendered to Professor Huguier.

I wasn't careful for long, and six months after the operation and the subsequent miscarriage I found myself pregnant again. My "sound constitution," I suppose, did the rest. Why was I in such a hurry?

I wanted everything. I wanted to be wife, mother, and lover, and I wanted everyone to know it, in the impatient pursuit that possessed me of some achievement or revelation, which might have been a desire to write but which was first of all a child.

I thought I had hold of the man of my life. I made his youth a source of pride: the men I'd been in love with before had been older—I'd imposed on them disastrous resemblances to my brothers, and they'd fled. Rather than trying to understand why, I buried myself in self-reproach, suffering from "not being loved," convinced that I never would be.

I was less frightened by this tormented young man. If he was incapable of saying "I love you," I felt I had the strength to teach him how, to transform him into that other I thought I saw in him: a mythical, passionate lover. I was asking too much of his few years and casting him in a role that the beginner he was could hardly assume.

Wanting to have a child is disconcerting. It was a desire I felt simply and violently. It seemed as inseparable from love as love was from sexual attraction.

What I see today is that this longing for a child suggests

a purely feminine kind of egotism. Faced with so strong and irrepressible a will to love, the poor male has no choice: he can only submit, vanquished by a desire that no longer corresponds to his own. —As I write this, I feel my praying mantis's antennae quiver!

Expecting a child was, on two occasions, a sensation that filled me with jubilation during the few months it possessed me. An impression—an illusion?—of attaining an absolute truth, of being with and within the essence of life.

Nostalgia for that condition overwhelms me. I remember so well the pleasure of carrying the child, being one with it in a state of intense, physical joy: unique moments where nothing else exists, neither fear nor anyone else outside of this double life that one proudly drags around. A pleasure that cannot be described.

It's in my mind alone that I remember that condition today—in words, sometimes in tears at having lost its secret. The empty shell of my aging body has inexorably forgotten it.

In 1969 we weren't informed of the sex of the fetus, which until its birth will simply be "the child," an object of wonder that I'll believe when I see it.

My previous two months were spent in bed: that was to be our honeymoon, behind the closed shutters of an apartment near Porte de Saint-Cloud that directly overlooked the construction site of the beltway. That was some summer—an ongoing scorcher, the complete works of Dostoyevsky, and the first man on the moon. I find my white skin slightly offensive—I so like turning golden in the sun—but I stare in wonder at my body as it loses its shape, without a care for its effect on my young husband.

Aside from reading and TV, we spend our time playing Scrabble in the breeze of electric fans. We make love frequently, quite imprudently, and with no concern for what our child might think: in the shelter of its bouncing balloon, it can only be delighted by the amorous exploits of its begetters.

I'm immersed in an irrational, utopian well-being, worrying neither about the future nor the present nor whatever he, the father, may apprehend about his role as father . . . My longing for the child and for its blissful fruition have possessed me completely. I've been transformed into an egg about to hatch in an overheated hothouse, a thousand miles away from all reality. We can go to the moon, after all . . .

Émilie was born at eight-and-a-half months on September 1st, the date chosen for the premature cesarean. For the rest of my life a moment in the pink bedroom of the Clinique Blomet will convey the strangest, most surreal feeling I ever experienced, except for certain dreams (but they were dreams): the moment when I woke from the anesthesia and heard the crying of a child I hadn't yet seen or held, with Jean-François's voice at my ear saying "It's a little girl," the cries of this child that was mine but no longer me. Without my knowing it, Émilie had already begun living, alone, apart from me: an inevitable sundering that was the miracle's flip side.

Without a care

On September 2, 1974—five years later almost to the day—I gave birth to my second daughter, an enigmatic little blonde called Léonore. I had carried her in the same state of euphoria, unawares of the perils of the outside world swirling and twisting around my rotundity, paying them no attention as I sailed along on my cloud.

Between the two children, our life has changed completely. My mother died in December, 1971. Grief mingled strangely with a longing to fly away: I was brimming with energy, with no other desire than to shed my skin and cast my moorings. Why stay in Paris when we were dreaming of nature and the open sea?

I've just written a dozen pages that came out of nowhere. Instinctively I know they contain the kernel of a book—the story that Nicole had been urging me to write in 1964.

Everything falls into place. Jean-François has given up his dreams of the theater to start writing articles, reviews, and a commissioned book. By chanced he meets an oddball who happens to own several houses in the south of France. One of them can be rented for six months in Val de Gilly, a lovely hamlet in the heart of the Maures hills. You can hear the murmur of a brook—in 1971 it's still a calm and happy place.

My mother has left me a little money, luckily not enough to buy a farm and a flock of sheep but enough to fritter away happily over two or three carefree years. In Paris we get rid of all we can, amid condescending looks ("Youth will have its fling"), especially after I announce that I'm going away in order to write a book. "She's out of her mind—she'll get over it." We pack our few possessions into cartons, give them away right and left, sell the rest, and throw away our worn-out clothes.

On a spring morning in 1972 we set off in an old Citroën Dyane overloaded with indispensable gear (such as our favorite books and records), as well as little Émilie, gleefully perched on a pile of sheets.

Our six months were transformed into two years spent in various houses in the area. I finished my book there, with the support and encouragement of Jean-François and Nicole, my demanding first readers, then, when things had become serious and official, of François-Régis Bastide at Éditions du Seuil.

Thirty years later, I regret nothing about our Bohemian life, those years when we played at being hippies on the Maures hillsides, listening to the Beatles, Verdi, Mahler, and the Who, watching in astonishment as we earned our freedom.

We'd had children together, but not the same expectations. Did we know it already? He wanted to roam the world, get to know other lands and other bodies with which to explore his anxieties. Today I can't blame him for that, even if it made me suffer at the time. I myself had not the least wish to discover another world: I'd found my very own and sat on the edge of my well listening to the sound of the stones I tossed into it.

I loved him. It was from and with him that I wanted a first child, then a second. I never imagined another life. I loved him; that was not enough. I was jealous and terrified at the thought of his leaving. But it was I who left him.

Did I thrust the role of father on him unfairly, the proof I demanded of his own love? Just as I had thrust marriage on him in my Victoire dress? On him so young, so unready to "start a family?"

And I, poor innocent that I was, the survivor of a shattered family, did I imagine I was starting anything at all? No, not in those terms; but all the same . . . Like a hardworking, devoted, stubborn insect I was constructing my indispensable cocoon and with the help of my charming male (how could I have

managed without him?) steadfastly depositing in it my precious eggs.

We were careful not to call it a family, in those times we
thought of as new, but it resembled one the way one honey-
comb cell resembles another; and a family it would well and
truly become at the moment of our separation—the moment
that I, the wicked female, would choose to take back everything I had tried to give you.

We spent eight years together without finding time to form
a couple. Its image haunted us, you as well as me. We were
both children of heartbreaking, heartbroken couples, we hardly
knew who we were, having survived oppressive silences, as yet
incapable of naming all the sorrows that had fashioned us and
driven us together.

We failed. We must stop blaming each other for that.

Time to form a couple

It's irresistible. Haunted by parental examples we want to avoid, we believe we're creating a new model, someplace else, far from the ghosts of childhood; and we find instead that we've constructed an environment whose dimensions scarcely differ from the one we've fled.

We dream of a nameless family that will in no way resemble the one we grew up in; we dream of raising our children safe from the injustices we endured or thought we endured, sparing them our ill-healed wounds while inflicting new and subtler ones on them with a perfectly clear conscience.

It's irresistible and pathetic. Sometimes, wearing their desires on their sleeves, dreams meet, walk together a little while, then break apart. It's been the same old song since the dawn of time.

What I see today in the potential young mother of 1968 and her passionate longing for a child is a dream: that of bringing together what in the obscure depths of her memory had always been separate, with the strange presumption that she could reunite in herself the masculine and the feminine that as father and mother she had always known apart. The dream of passionately wanting to reconcile in her own womb the two stray beings that had been her parents. Of persuading herself that her own birth hadn't been due simply to a hurried chance reunion one day in May, 1941. Of passionately wishing that on that day they still loved one another.

A couple

About a year after the publication of *The Laurels* I received a letter from one Jacques P. in Mexico. He'd read the article in *Le Monde* that Jacqueline Piatier had devoted to my book. He was intrigued and set about obtaining a copy, something that took a little while.

In his letter he said he believed, was in fact almost certain that he had identified the character named Albert B., whom as a young man he'd heard about privately. He felt he was in possession of certain clues that would lead to a "revelation" that was likely to upset as well as interest me. At all costs he wished to be discreet and so was waiting for my reaction to his letter before proceeding further.

My curiosity aroused, I replied at once and three weeks later received a thick registered special-delivery envelope containing some twenty pages, Xeroxed from the cross-ruled pages of a spiral notebook: excerpts from a diary my correspondent had kept from his early years. They concerned the summer of 1941, when he was seventeen and spending his vacation in the countryside not far from Lyons.

The weather's warm; no mention is made of the distant war; life seems easy for a bunch of carefree youngsters who split their leisure time between picnics and bicycle rides. Evenings they gather for orangeade or *diabolo menthe* at the amiable family hotel, where the anglers who are its regulars take their meals.

One day they are intrigued by a new arrival, a woman apparently older than they are, maybe twenty. She sits by herself with her soda in front of her, buried in a book she doesn't seem to be reading. Jacques immediately falls in love with her. On the third evening he risks approaching the mysterious young woman, so sad-looking, he writes, that she can only be hiding something . . .

She acts slightly aloof, albeit "perfectly nice, as though she were dealing with a child." Then less aloof: she finally agrees to slip away into the fields, just the two of them, or bicycle along the little paths lined with willows.

She takes trips to Lyons, where she spends several days before returning. At the end of two weeks he still knows no more of her than the scent of lily of the valley on her upswept hair and frizzy nape, and the kiss he finally manages to steal from her. She agrees to answer his increasingly insistent questions, then tells him that this kiss will be the last. She cries a while before confiding in him, fiddling with a blade of grass, next to the bikes they've laid on their sides by the path.

First of all, she's married—yes, married, young as she is, not yet twenty-one, but it's not that; she doesn't love her husband, thank heavens he travels a lot and she gets away from him whenever she can—he's close to her parents, they're the ones who "forced her to marry him."

How could such a thing . . . ? They're strict, she was a minor, they felt she was heading for trouble and needed settling down. At eighteen, without their knowing it, she'd joined the youth organization of the PPF, Jacques Doriot's party. Nothing scared her, and she often volunteered to join the "shock troops" who were sent into communist rallies as spoilers and were beaten off with fists and stones. Once, shots had even been fired.

This had greatly displeased her parents, respectable shop-keepers that they were, as well as their customers. They saw marriage as the only way to calm her down. She'd given in to their pressure.

That's not all. In fact she doesn't give a damn about politics, the war, even the Germans. She has a secret: she loves an older man, one twice her age, someone "high up" in Doriot's party. His name is Albert Beugras. She's been his mistress for two years, still is, now that she's married, and no one else knows.

Their relationship keeps getting more and more complicated. He himself has a wife and three children—a whole family. He also says that his love for her, Raymonde, will overcome every obstacle. But how? The situation makes her very unhappy, but she can't contemplate giving him up.

Several days go by. Raymonde comes back from Lyons despondent. She needs to talk to the young man. "You're my only friend." She starts crying. Life is so unfair . . . She's now sure that she's pregnant, and not by her husband, and there it is.

Appalled, Jacques asks, "What are you planning to do?"

"I don't know. My lover keeps begging me to have the baby, which is pure madness. He can't leave his wife. Anyway, I'm married. If this child is born, dear Jacques, there'll be only the three of us who'll know who the father is."

After this confession Raymonde disappears from the young man's life. He's tried everything to find her, during the war and after. He's never seen her since. She may not even have told him her real name.

By comparing the precise dates in this diary with those of my parents' lives (and that of my own birth), it's easy to see that my father got young Raymonde pregnant at exactly the same time as I was conceived.

When the letter from Mexico reached me with its revelations, Juliette was still alive. I spoke to her about it, cautiously, realizing that I was the one who was afraid of learning more.

Hands deep in her apron pockets, she shook her head and raised her eyes to the ceiling.

"My poor darling! Your father . . . your poor mother. I never heard of this Raymonde. There were others . . ."

"She knew?"

"She didn't want to know, for heaven's sake! What could she do? She adored him. She endured what had to be endured. And then we had other fish to fry. '41, '42—it was getting worse and worse. If we'd known what was in store for us over the next ten years!"

The "family mystery" has never been solved. Once I'd heard it, I bragged about it whenever I had the chance. I was amused by this notion of a potential twin brother. Not anymore. I think of her and hear her weeping. And I can't forgive him for this particular betrayal. Even if I still hear something else Juliette said, hoping to put an end to the matter: "Don't be too curious. At that time, you know, this happened in every decent family. People didn't leave each other for such trifles."

The Summer of the Elder Tree—I
(Diary: excerpts)

Paris, June 14, 2000

I join Émilie and César at Saint-Sulpice. He's coming shopping with me. He's so sweet, this little boy with his serious look. He makes me so sad, with a whole paradise lost already behind him. It's hard for me to make my way in this new state of affairs—the breakup of Richard-Émilie, the "it's all over." Everything's there and no longer there. The same and not the same.

Evening (8 P.M.)

Émilie and I go on foot to Bureau Lane at 170 Rue de Charonne. There, in a little theater called The Proscenium, Léo and four other actors are performing J. C. Grumbert's play, *Dirty Laundry*. It fits right in.

Émilie is very beautiful, dazzling, and seems sure of her beauty. My feeling: "I don't understand her." Had I been like her? Why keep looking for resemblances all the time? Comparing us, observing us, looking for "me" in my daughter? Why this wish to "understand"? I sense that she's both at loose ends and extremely determined. No regrets; talking about divorce as she fixes her makeup; impassive. They're already so separated.

(On a loose sheet)
And yet you've been here before
    love's absence
in the place exactly
    the same place

where love was so alive
   so dense
   so unquestionable

Abruptly an empty place
   a hollow
like the place left
   in the hollowed pillow
   by the cat
that such a short time before
filled it with all its weight
with all its heat
   compact and soft

Or like the egg's place
   in the straw
   still warm
You could touch
   that warmth
   with the back of your hand

But abruptly a void
   love's no longer there
it's incomprehensible
as sudden and irremediable
   as the cat that jumped away
   no longer there
   that's all

A new love
   lies in wait for that place
   and will take it.
It's frightening, isn't it?

You've been here before
there's nothing you can do.

Paris, June 24

A little red devil (pajamas) is sleeping in the green bedroom at the end of the corridor. I've just been lavishing kisses on him. He smelled sweet. He reminds me of my own two crazy little children: nothing made me secretly happier than to watch them while they slept, my mind at rest in knowing them there, with me. Nothing bad could happen to them, sheltered as we were, together under the same roof. While elsewhere . . . the immense world . . .

Lans-en Vercors, June 28

At my table, facing the window. Bad weather—clouds and wind—but in this part of the country, toward end of day, the sky always does its best to wash itself clean and let the sun splash over the greenness, over the fields.

We'd arrived Monday the 26th on such a beautiful day, a blessing. Happier than ever to get out of Paris. Up here, surprised by the blaze of our peonies, their heads all turned toward us. The vast, magnificent elder has recovered its beauty—a plump, lace-bedecked bride. The Virginia creeper is making its way through the front door. Birdsong. Calm. Delicious weariness after a bottle of Mercurey. Just the two of us, at last. I collapse, barely hearing, before sleep comes, the sound of the piano in the night . . .

Lans, July 5, 11 P.M.

Behind the green shutters on the upper floor a little boy

is sleeping. Below, in the living room, is a passably dejected grandmother, her heart in tatters the last two days, suffering from stomach pains as well, which are plainly "nervous." Whenever I can't fall asleep, I cry like a fool.

At one point yesterday, while busy in the midst of his trucks, tractors, and other machines, the boy said: "You know what Papa says when there's big trouble? He says, 'We're in deep shit!'" Then he bursts out laughing.

Feeling so downcast. Is it the boy's arrival alone? The empty house across the way, the "guest house" that each summer had become their own? I haven't set foot in it. Images from that time, happiness of that time, the old days, when everyone loved everyone else . . .

Sad sentimental grandmother!

I think I loved Richard and his crazy ways too much. I totally relied on him, on his strength and intelligence and heart. Is part of me angry with Émilie? For not having kept her own word when she said, "I love him, I'll never leave him"?

Waves of the elder's sweetish scent reach me through the window and mingle with the scorched smell of stupid moths ending their days on the halogen bulb. "It's a disaster!" as César says when he spills yoghurt over his knees.

Saturday evening, July 8

Alone in the main house with the boy asleep in the next room and Lulu the cat on my feet. A disagreeable awakening at 5:30. Wind and rain.

I begin turning things over in my mind—images, places, endings. The impression of being in a "real life" plagiary of Chekhov, in the melancholy of a house one has to abandon. Once again I think of the snapshots taken last year at summer's end. I'm alone with them. We'd lunched on the green iron table in front of the guesthouse in the shade of the walnut tree. They'd always said "walnut-tree shadow is bad," without ever explaining quite why. Maybe it's my beloved walnut tree that's the cause of all this? The light was shimmering so beautifully that I photographed the three of them, the child and the couple, so intimate, so tender, with the shadow of leaves traced on their faces. Thinking about it in the early hours devastates me. The light was too golden, movingly precise, fatal.

A little later, as he drank his Ovaltine in the kitchen, César was watching the shredded white mist that mottled the landscape: "Marie, look, there's dust on the trees."

I finally spoke to Martine, while she was straightening the bedspread—with an (absurd) feeling of stage fright, of having to confess to the separation (to my very own Martine, who's known the family for fifteen years!) as if it were a shameful aberration. Her reaction, calm and normal (I'm the one who's not normal): "Marie, they should know what they're doing. It's their life."

(Correlation:)

Why do I feel so uneasy speaking "behind the innocent child's back" of what's being planned without his knowing it? It doesn't take me long to recognize my own embarrassment and sadness as a child whenever my mother felt obliged to "discuss the situation," which was as follows:

After his trial in 1948 led to a verdict of life imprisonment, my father served his sentence in the prison at Fresnes. Our family was living in Uncle Pierre's gray house in Suresnes. In the friendly neighborhood of Upper Suresnes we never sensed any malice. For the two oldest children in the lycée, things were different. My brother Paul was obliged to change schools several times. My sister Anne and I found a refuge among the Dominican nuns of the Institut Saint Pie X in Saint-Cloud, a private institution patronized by the daughters of respectable bourgeois families. It wasn't all roses (one pious family intervened to demand the expulsion of "that collaborationist's daughters") but in general we were happy enough.* We were cautioned (especially me, the little girl) to "say nothing." For instance, to the question "What does your father do?" we were not to answer "He's in jail" but "He's a chemical engineer," nothing more. In any case, I never was much of a talker.

I understood later that my mother's worst ordeals were the invitations to my classmates' homes. She had no wish to deprive me of them—the main thing was for me to feel "like everybody else"—but what a price she must have paid! She went with me into these lovely villas, and I watched her as she took the mother who'd invited me aside and "talked to her." I never asked her what she said, but "I knew." My poor mother, beautiful and erect in her threadbare black suit, swallowing her pride and her distress as she tried to explain in her politest manner that even with a collaborationist father in prison, I was a worthy to be received by the respectable folk of Saint-Cloud and Val d'Or.

Places must become imbued with emotions and sorrows that resurface years later: this house, for instance, so welcoming now, scared me out of my wits when I moved into it twenty-four years ago with Harry and my two daughters. He'd bought the property in 1958, with its three houses, the same as in *Goldilocks*: one big, one middle-sized, one small.

---

* The headmistress of Saint Pie X was a beautiful and remarkable woman and the sister of Colonel Rémy, the great resistance fighter.

The first early September I spent there was rainy and buffeted by the south wind. Harry had had to meet his parents in Italy for a trip planned long before, the telephone was out of order, I was in despair with my little girls now separated from their father, left alone in the midst of angry gusts and an old farm that grated and creaked, its noises making my heart shudder. I bewailed the failure of my marriage and the ending of love stories that drag on in mourning for what one couldn't make last. This evening I remember that "passage" from one life to another as a precipitous footbridge swaying above a jungle . . .

Such a touchy little boy! Hard put to resist him; afraid of upsetting him. A while ago I hurt his feelings by saying "That's enough meows for now!" because he'd been playing cat and I'd had all the meowing I could take. He burst into inconsolable tears. I no longer knew what to do: he just kept pushing me away. I kept saying how sorry I was . . . What a miserable teacher of grandchildren I am!

Still in Lans, Monday, July 10

All is calm when I go to bed. In silvery half-moon light the elder tree is cloaked in its mantilla: immense flowers gradually losing their florets as they're expelled by the pinheads of green berries.

The great umbels take on an aspect of embroidered netting. Tarlatan; the under-wiring of petticoats; gentle mesh strewn with spangles. A few days ago the umbels were heavy with their unctuous ivory whiteness, lace for wasp-waisted brides. Now they are all thinning, soon to grow heavy again with garnet-colored fruit.

Late April: Émilie arrives

Her emotion on the station platform when she sees her little boy again. In a dither. Restless as a puppy. "I'm in love," she whispers. I'm stiff as a poker: "Already?"

We get together after dinner, once the boy is in bed. Her lovely eyes mist over: she sees all too clearly I'm in the dumps. Everything's gone so quickly, I have a hard time keeping up. She knows it. I love her. We've always loved each other, heart-rendingly, my daughters and I, even if we forgot to say so (in fact we didn't forget), even when I abandoned them on my long-distance trips (at least I think so). Her first question:

"Are you angry with me?"

"Yes, I'm angry with you. A little bit. There, it's out, I'm not angry anymore."

And that's true.

Stones that weigh down the heart shouldn't be thrown like stones—it's too painful, and they can kill. They must be transformed into words and passed back and forth. Speaking, using language. You and I, my darling, know a few things about words. We've always talked to one another, without telling lies. What's hurting me belongs to me; regrets are my very own; the sorrow that overwhelms me, forget it, it will fly away with the wild geese, it will go join the others in the land of old times, where they'll keep each other warm. Don't worry about it.

This pain that is all mine has come from far away. It looks at me with curious eyes, wondering how I'm going to appease it.

You did the same thing

Spring, 1976

Funny how certain memories acquire a photographic precision. I'm looking at my kohl-ringed eyes in the rearview mirror of a Volkswagen camper I've parked in a lot on the outskirts of Sainte-Maxime. I'm alone. I say, as if I were addressing someone else, "In any case, separation is inevitable."

In this cool spring I'm wearing a long-sleeved blouse, its black fabric printed with tiny blue, violet, and mauve flowers. My waistcoat of padded cotton is bordered with the same fabric.

I'm thirty-four years old, my long hair has a reddish henna sheen, there's the scent of sandalwood on my tanned skin. I've just decided to leave my husband, my handsome young man whose hair has a reddish henna sheen.

In my mind, it was at this very moment that everything got under way. My newfound freedom: the possibility of leaving the man I'd loved, whom I still loved, for the lover who had suddenly appeared a few weeks earlier and whom—incapable as I am of living two loves at the same time—I'm now designating as the man of my life.

I'm good-looking, I'm successful. My second book has just appeared, a love letter to my late mother. In a matter of seconds, unhesitatingly, I break up my family.

I have the impression (I remember exactly the inordinate strength that I felt growing inside me) that I'm a bulldozer slowly starting up: I'm on my way and nothing will stop me. The image of a bulldozer may not be very romantic, but it's what came to me.

Émilie isn't quite seven years old, Léonore almost two. I turned them into children of separated parents. I decided this all by myself, at the controls of my bulldozer, at the wheel of our red camper, a mythical vehicle of the hippy and post-hippy eras in which we wandered about for several years, taking our mobile home around Europe loaded with children and friends, in long hair and printed cotton skirts, with bidis and joints . . . Today the dream is shattered.

At this precise moment that determined my life, and not only my own, I have no recollection of assessing the harm that my decision might entail. A deliberate separation is an act of inevitable cruelty. It's me first, my life before yours, and we'll see what happens. I don't recall a single qualm.

Summer 2000

While I keep mulling over my sadness and ways of escaping from it by filling up page after page of this notebook, Léonore (aged twenty-five) gives me an opportune jolt:

"You shouldn't get so involved in their problems."

"Thanks for the advice."

"And anyway" (getting irritated on the phone) "do you realize how old I was when you did it to me? I was a baby who didn't even know how to talk! You didn't explain anything to us. We found ourselves in a house, and there you were in a bed with another man."

The dream is shattered

Summer 1976

That morning I left. A cool, mild September morning. We had given up Val de Gilly and were living in a somewhat decrepit but pleasant house whose front faced Place du Cros in Grimaud. You walked straight off the street through a glass door into what had formerly been a shop. In the single, long, ground-floor room that ended in a damp cave hewn out of the rock, the only window was the shop window, its top forming an arc. I'd hung it with lengths of lace bought second-hand at the Saint-Tropez market. A steep stone stairway wound its way up to the two second-floor bedrooms.

Our bedroom window looked out on the square with its narrow old houses and on the fragrant bakery, next to the steps where old Madeleine used to sit in black dress and apron, her snow-white hair coiled into a tiny bun. She spent the best part of the day chatting with neighbors and joking about her toothless mouth with the children who kept climbing onto her knees.

Exuberant wisteria overran the façade, its inquisitive tentacles crept into the window aperture—that summer we'd given up trying to shut it completely, remember? The fine white voile of the closed curtain kept catching on the leaves when it moved.

That morning I got up early to leave—to leave you. The children were at their grandparents' near Aix-en-Provence.

Straight and still as a log, your hands crossed behind your head, you incredulously watch me scurrying about: "You're really going?"

How did I manage it? I remember only the following sequence:

Place de Cros is deserted, Madeleine isn't yet seated on the steps, the smell of the first loaves of olive bread floats in the air. I'm at the wheel of the red camper, my foot on the brake, ready to go down the little street that leads to the grocer's, then after a hairpin turn runs alongside the Café de France. I turn around one last time, leaning my head, arm, and shoulder out the open window. I raise my arm to wave to you. Bare-chested, emerging from the wisteria, you make a little gesture, wiggling your fingers. I release the brake, your face is in the rearview mirror, I leave thinking: I'm crazy.

That morning the road leads toward Nice, then Italy. I have an appointment on the station square in Genoa with my American lover, who has come by train from Venice. We're supposed to have lunch in Genoa, then drive together to Venice, which he's giving up for me—Venice where a woman lives whom he still loves and whom he is also about to leave. We're crazy.

On the autoroute where I tear along from bridge to tunnel, it suddenly crushes me: the magnitude of what must be overturned and destroyed for the sole, perhaps illusory purpose of "starting a new life." It's a fine time to cry, it's over, it's too late to rekindle your longing for a love you weren't able to save. It's *over*. Cry if you like, but careful, it's starting to rain, don't fly off the road with your camper full of burned-out memories, there's someone waiting for you down the road.

Standing in the station square, the dashing lover all atremble with tenderness watched a bedraggled, puffy-faced, teary woman arrive. Ah, wasn't that worth the trip? The woman of his life was a real beauty.

You didn't explain anything to us

Early November 2000

Before leaving Paris to take up my period of residence in America (Harry and I divide our time between the United States and France), I was perusing my library in the hope of adding a few last volumes to the pile waiting to be mailed *par avion*. Among them was *L'autre livre* by Michel Butel.

Why hadn't I read this book when I'd bought it at its appearance in '97? It's odd: there are moments when books beckon to you and the words you find in them are the ones you need then and there.

In the section of this unusual book called "Autobiography," M. Butel devotes two pages to his sons: Ivan, born in May '68, and Stephen, born in May '69, the children of Catherine, with whom he is no longer living in 1975 when the incident he relates occurs:

"For Christmas I suggested they pick the most extraordinary and unreasonable present imaginable, and I would give it to them . . . They had forty-eight hours to make up their minds."

The children didn't dare say what they'd chosen.

"I almost lost my temper . . . They finally explained that they just wanted to see us wake up on Christmas morning in the same bed, her and me, because you see, Papa, we don't remember the two of you together . . ."

What a quick surge of empathy for Michel Butel! The memory comes back of an analogous scene of my own:

We're outside the Bon Marché, on the sidewalk of Rue du Bac, on a day during a school vacation when I'd come up to Paris with my two daughters (they were going to school in Villard-de-Lans), Léonore then six or seven, Émilie consequently eleven or twelve. We'd lunched with their father, the four of us had had "a good time together," and we were about to say good-bye. They kissed him, then he and I approached one another. From a yard away, Léo's voice: "A kiss on the lips!"

Our two heads together turned toward her. The expression on her face! Joy, provocation, and pure impishness intermingled.

"You mean it?"

With a radiant smile she whispers, "Yes!"

So the two separated parents do as they are told, embrace and kiss each other's lips, just like the movies.

Michel Butel ends his story:

"We gave them a lot of fabulous presents, but not that one. We weren't smart? I'd like to see you try it."

". . . see you try it"

Fall 1976
Lans-en-Vercors

The girls sleep in the same downstairs bedroom. Nights are restless. Léo, "still a two-and-a-half-year-old baby," wakes up in tears several times a night. Nothing new about that, it's been that way since her birth. I wake up gasping and ply her with bottles whose contents I keep changing; I don't know what to try—other than taking her into my bed, something rather tricky at present, even if the "new man" is unbelievably accommodating.

Tonight it's different. Léonore has fallen asleep. Not Émilic, who calls for me and begs me to stay with her so we can talk. She desperately wants to know "why we don't live with Papa anymore, all four of us the way we used to—poor Papa!"

How can one explain it? This absurd situation, this "over and done with," this paradise despoiled without their being consulted, this "never again?"

What explanation could measure up to the incongruity that separation signifies to a child? What words will ever justify the pain inflicted by the person—in this case her mother—who claims to love her above all?

That night, I'm sure I didn't evade the anguished questions of my little girl. She says she doesn't remember what I told her. She says that in fact that she suffers from the lack of specific memories of her early childhood.

What could I offer her besides motives that for her were totally inadequate and acceptable only because it was I, her mother, who imposed them on her, while demanding from her an absolute, tacit trust in me? I settle her in "another house," confront her with "another man in my bed," and thus abruptly oblige her to face the irreversible situations and sinister injustices of the adult world. What an abuse of power!

In exchange I declare my boundless mother's love. It's true that I've never been sure of anything except that same love, without making an ideal of it. I believe it's what kept us afloat, daughters and mother alike, a fragile flotilla made of scratch paper, until we found a provisional haven.

What happens is that we improvise, walking on eggshells, making up our own life and happiness, hoping with all the good will in the world that bits of them will be shared by our progeny. Later, much later, we look back over the landscape we've passed through, its ups and downs, its inevitable disparities, and we put up with it—not much to glory in, at best an accommodation. If I turn back today toward our family landscape, I can look at it without running away, with a few regrets, naturally, but not shame.

If I didn't "explain everything" to you, I believe I always "said" and "showed" without reserve, with the windows wide open. And no lies.

February 2001

On a Miami–Paris flight I most opportunely come across a *Paris-Match* article about a couple of so-called celebrities. I don't think it inappropriate to reprint its main point here:

". . . Both have led lives of their own. Detached from their pasts, they are the very image of a family reconstituted in a spirit of gentleness . . . Both lived through the pain of a breakup in the past year. Each of them succeeded in avoiding the dramas of separation that used to seem inevitable. But at thirty-four they belong to a generation that accepts that love doesn't always mean forever, that love affairs can be tender rather than stormy, a generation that rightly favors the equilibrium of children. She has two daughters and he a little son. A. and E. are perhaps the emblem of a new way of loving."

Isn't separation a true fairy tale that is beginning to take root as a social and generational phenomenon? People may marry or not, but many do get married, they have children, they separate, they remarry, they bring along their children from one family to the next, they mix them together, they add "halves" to them one after the other and isn't it wonderful?!

And no lies

Several years after the appearance of my first book, an inventory of the family disaster in which I'd set down my roots, a woman my age got in touch with me, hoping we could meet. She too was trying to write a book about her father, who had left behind a diary and some documents.

The daughter of one of my father's comrades-in-arms (those benighted arms brandished in the collaborationist camp). She wanted to talk to me about them, wondering "how I'd extricated myself so soon" by publishing my book.

The same political party (Jacques Doriot's PPF), the same involvement, the same crazy illusions had led them both to the same prison in Fresnes after the war. Less compromised than my father, judged less severely, hers had spent "less time inside," she said, two or three years all the same, during which the little girls went to see him on Saturday, which was visitors' day; maybe not *every* Saturday the way we, my father's children, used to do, but often enough, believing all the time that she was going to see him in a hospital.

"What do you mean, in a hospital?"

Riveted to the sofa, I contemplated this apparently normal woman, bewildered by the incredible, stifling lie that a mother crazed by anxiety and shame had imposed on her.

"Yes, Mama used to say that Papa was in a hospital. I'd never seen a hospital—I believed her."

"Oh—and when he got out?"

"Well, I suppose I assumed he was cured. It wasn't till much later . . . Anyway, they're both dead, and I'm still in analysis."

"I see."

A case of nervous giggles started working its way up from my navel. I kept it under control, thank heaven, staring hard at the patterns in a kilim. I no longer remember how the visit ended; I've blanked it out.

The next news I had of the innocent visitor of Fresnes was on an October afternoon in 2001. She called me; we spoke at length on the phone. Her book was coming along. I talked to her again about "the hospital" and asked if she would authorize my using the episode in a story.

"Of course," she said.

Then the plot thickened:

"I talk about it in my own book. Did I make it clear that sometimes I was allowed to go and give my father a kiss?"

"I don't think so."

"There was a room at the far end of the visitors lounge. A guard would open the door and I'd race through it and throw myself into the arms of this beloved man who looked perfectly healthy to me. What I didn't understand was why my mother wasn't permitted to come with me."

"And—?"

"She explained that his disease was one that only grown-ups could catch."

Fresnes Hospital

In 2000, at the height of summer, the official report on French prisons and prison life was made public. Adjectives blossomed in the written and spoken media, as well they might: appalling, unimaginable, monstrous, etc.

In my opinion, the most eloquent report was a photographic supplement published in *Libération*. The power of its images in black and white, or rather gray and gray, ranging from dirty to sooty by way of grimy, made you truly see the dilapidation of the premises. See and smell.

I recognized these crumbling corridors, where the stench of urine vied with the huge overflowing soup tureens rattling around on their carts making a racket like that of a switching yard. These same genuine late-'40s corridors down which a little girl used to caper on her Saturday outings, dressed to the nines with white socks and a bow in her hair, forbidden to take off her gloves or go near the rusting iron banisters. So as to avoid the foul latrines, our mother didn't let us drink from early morning on. Every so often one still had to go into them to throw up.

The visitors' lounges do seem to show signs of improvement. In one very dark and blurry photograph in the same supplement, I think I can make out a couple "half" embracing—I mean that only the upper parts of their bodies touch, some obscure kind of furniture preventing more intimate contact.

In my time, which was above all my parents' time, there was no chance of touching. The visitors' lounge I knew, in the so-called "political prisoners" wing at Fresnes, was a place designed to impose absolute separateness. Two rows of stalls faced one another: on one side the prisoners, each in his cage, on the other their families crammed in in varying numbers, in our case my mama, my brother and sister. We couldn't budge. We had to leave the door open whenever my grandfather came (rarely). The holes in the mesh that enclosed these cubicles from the ceiling to a kind of little wall where I used to sit sideways— these holes wouldn't even let one of my gloved fingers through them. Between the two rows of cages a guard walked up and down, never stopping during the entire time of our visit, which as I remember lasted twenty to thirty screaming minutes. A bell would ring, followed by sighs and brief sobbing. The sound of bolts on the prisoners' side. "Time's up!" one of the bulls would cry. We had to get out—another batch was pushing its way in from the section landing. Some hospital.

I'm not looking for pity, only saying that I've seen these images of prison misery for too long and that in the two-thousandth year after Jesus Christ it may be time to do something.

And let me add that our mother, dressed every Saturday in her finest two-piece suit, under the mask of a seductive woman with finishing touches of glamorous lipstick, rice powder, and Cinq de Molyneux, our sweet mother, beside herself with love and hope, never showed any fear or shame in displaying her jailed husband to her children. We will always be beholden to her for the lies she spared us. Even if, during the years of separation, she didn't explain very much, she didn't hide anything either. Her mute courage and the strength of the love that she radiated were my bedrock.

Did she have faith enough in us to let us be responsible for our own emotions? It's possible. In any case, without my being aware of it, she necessarily set herself, by her behavior, as the example we should follow "so as not to lie." An example as silent as an icon, shedding her tears only at night so as not to frighten the children . . . Did she think we couldn't hear her? Did she think that by winnowing her rare revelations, by describing my father as a victim, as the scapegoat of a fatal conflict that was beyond our control (among other clichés), did she believe that there was a chance we wouldn't need to know more, one day?

An example in spite of everything, an adored motherly icon whose silences were so eloquent that once I was old enough to hear them, I had only transcribe their unspoken meanings.

. . . her tears only at night

My parents died a long time ago; my father in 1963, my mother in 1971. Writing down dates is hard. I make myself do it. Dating an event is like a slap, "it wakes you up," Juliette would have said—Juliette who showered our young years with common sense.

During all the time that bars and distance separated them— seven years of absolute separation—they wrote each other every day. During the Fresnes years, I remember seeing pages of poor-quality paper arrive blackened by my father's tiny handwriting, with lines and paragraphs crossed out with red or blue and with crayon markings (it must have been the first time that I heard the word "censorship"), each page smeared with the heavy, sloppy stamp of "Fresnes Prison." So as to conceal a few more words of love?

I imagine the pleasure (or boredom) of the professional stamper, I see fingers yellowed with nicotine and the waxy cuffs of a uniform.

I never read these letters, hundreds and thousands of them. After my mother's death, I asked Juliette, who had lived with her to the end. She quietly answered:

"She destroyed everything a few months ago. I didn't stop her. I think she did the right thing."

Usually my memory is reliable. In this case I can't recall the exact moment when Juliette told me this; I don't remember how I felt. I know that she told me this as a fact, a clear answer to my question. That was Juliette all over: "She did it, that's all. That's the way it is. Let's forget it."

Thinking back on it, as I write this, a shudder rises from some depth and affects my hand as it moves across the page.

I reenact the scene:

" . . . I think she did the right thing."

"Of course, she did the right thing."

How could I swallow that without screaming, without spitting up the lump of charred silences that Juliette was trying to make me keep down? If I'd at least shouted: "Did the proper thing? You're crazy! You let her burn up ten years of their life? Their only life 'together'? Those letters were the one link that existed between two isolated and wretched people."

"You're the one who's crazy! Did you want to be stuck with their misery? And their regrets?"

If I close my eyes I see ruins, the scene of a romantic château as it collapses, half-burned pages taking flight from a nest of ashes; I hear the rustle of wings against a cavern's walls, the sound of sobbing.

She did the right thing—she destroyed everything, it was her wish and her choice. Did she burn the secrets of their divided union to spare us, the two surviving daughters, now that both our brothers were dead?

Today the shudder speaks to me and dictates this: if she hadn't done it, perhaps I would have never dared write. In order to spare them, my parents, who were for so many years unable to hear or speak?

Reunion

In the summer of 1953 my father recovered his freedom, benefiting from a commutation of his sentence, a result of President Vincent Auriol's amnesty of collaborators still in prison at that time.

He had spent the last months of his captivity teaching chemistry and math at a camp for juvenile delinquents in Oermingen, Lorraine. Nowadays we would call it a "center" rather than a "camp."

The whole family (at least what's left of it) has come to collect its amnestied prisoner at the "camp" entrance. That includes my mother, of course, aged forty-nine; my brother, Paul, twenty-four; my sister, Anne, nineteen; me, a child of eleven; as well as Louis, my grandfather, still handsome at seventy-nine. He has provided the means of transportation, his gleaming Citroen 15CV, to carry off these fine people quivering with emotion.

Against a background of the bleak plains of Lorraine and coils of barbed wire piled up into walls, here is another interesting photograph, which doesn't exist but which I remember as if I'd taken it. A photograph or a home movie.

It's hot. It's mid afternoon. He's coming calmly toward us, in dark trousers and a light-colored short-sleeved shirt open at the collar, a cigarette between his lips, a suitcase in one hand and packages in the other.

Greeted by the guard, he walks through the gate, sets his luggage down, throws away his butt, takes a deep breath. Nods to his impassive father and goes to him first for a silent, manly embrace. Then turns to us, two petrified children glued to the spot. He presses us to his breast, one after the other. (Does he tell himself, "One of them's missing?") My heart is in my boots.

Does he pick me up? No, I'm already tall—"a beanpole," says my brother. And tears? No, we know how to behave. We've learned.

And what about her—standing stiffly to one side, in her thin dress adorned with poppies, cornflowers, and ears of wheat? She . . . I had to lower my eyes to avoid disturbing their embrace, the first in nine years, since that summer night in Paris in 1944 when he fled with Jean.

I don't hear the suppressed sob or their breath coming faster, but I imagine their confusion, their effort not to let the other sense the upheaval of physical contact, not show their feelings from the assembled family. Tears of joy? There were none.

While he keeps her in his arms, does he murmur in her ear, "I'm back, it's over"? or "I love you" or "You smell good"? or nothing at all? Does she think, close to fainting as she presses against him, "We'll start all over again, my love" or "It's too late"?

It took me years to reenact the scene, years to understand that these two—our parents—had never really come together again.

Anne and I who, keeping to ourselves, had brooded over our own pasts, swallowing the bitter tears of childhood, have only recently been able to talk about it, on the sly—as if the dead were waiting to surprise us and scold us for letting the secret out.

I don't dare think of their first night in that country hotel room. It pains me to remember the big-flowered wallpaper in the stairwell and the glumness that prevailed when we all forgathered the next morning, our noses in our tasteless cups of *café au lait*, unable to look at each other.

The game is over.

Both of them in their fifties: she, so in love, worn out by

forbearance, sleepless nights, and menopause; he, newly free, in the prime of life, "ten years down the drain" (fifteen if you count his political divagations). Does he tell himself, "I saved my skin, but now I have to start everything from scratch"?

And we children? Contemplating the disaster open-mouthed? Not yet. Write instead: dreaming of being elsewhere so as not to see them crack, wondering which one would be the first to go. Be brave, children, disaster will come later.

I don't resent them anymore. They did what they could, together and separately. Through ordeals and silences, they passed on what they had to pass on: love and separation.

Disaster

Less than three years after my father's return, my mother was struck down by a cerebral hemorrhage that left her a hemiplegic and a cripple for life at fifty-two.

Thus any possibility of reconciliation between these two destitute people, my parents, is cut short. Separated for years by the "force of circumstances," deceptively reunited by the divine goodness to which we appealed in our prayers, they are now again separated, forever.

It's a destabilizing, fatal shock to their marriage and our lives. What has happened to God in all of this?

She is the first to succumb. I'm fourteen. With her the world collapses—the walls of our house, our childhood, our joy. Nothing's left that is true or credible: the walls were made of cardboard, the roof that confined our childhood has blown away, joy has gone up in smoke.

Adolescence is no time for understanding or acceptance. I suffer more than I can tell: I'm the victim of a terrible betrayal. She whom I thought invincible, our own mother, the wise sorceress who possessed the potion of love, who raised up our ramparts out of her tears and knew what spell could keep the structure intact, who so valiantly kept every outside adversary at bay, could not resist the blow that would destroy her from within. We weren't present; we didn't see her succumb: she abandoned us.

We will never have had a normal life. First, a father gone elsewhere, and whose fault was that? And now our mother— what have we done to deserve a broken woman, stonily indifferent to our love?—gone elsewhere in turn.

A stifled adolescence. No rebelliousness for us: after being nice to the prisoner, you have to be nice to the invalid woman.

Keep your mouth shut and curse the fate that has taken God's place, since God is, they say, only goodness.

From '55 to '57 our family album is all mutilating gloom. Being abandoned has split us apart. We wander around like actors who have never rehearsed together, thrust onto a stage full of unfamiliar scenery and trap doors, having to perform a drama without knowing our lines. Bumping into each other, clenching our teeth in resentment, each trapped in a grief woven out of hatred.

Juliette is the only one who can keep a conversation going. She is the practical, all-powerful household divinity who makes sure we survive. Paul, my brother, has met the love of his life, and another family; he flees. He's right. He'll have a reprieve lasting a few short years—a well-deserved one, people will say—before he also succumbs, a wreck.

My father? Hard to say: he's impenetrable. Is he suffering? He must be. From time to time he blows his top, and I watch the bear that's gotten out of his cage. On evenings when he comes home late, I can't sleep and wait for the sound of a key in the lock. Through the half-open door of my bedroom I size him up at a glance: a sad and tired old man impregnated with alcohol and tobacco. He's fifty-three or fifty-four. It's awful.

One night his haggard face is blotched with lipstick. I'm ashamed for him without really knowing why. Today I'd shed tears of pity for him.

What has kept me going are the routine of whispered breakfasts in the kitchen with Juliette, the routine of my beloved lycée, the stupefying revelation of literature and the theater, and above all else my sister.

During the months when my mother lies supine and inert, it is Anne, the closest to her, who tries to explain to me the mysteries of this bisected woman: so that I can be less frightened, be capable of recognizing the first signs of hope. Eight years my elder, my sister becomes the maternal go-between who provides the only salutary shelter, that of love.

Here is what I'm discovering this very moment as I write: I think we huddled together inside an essential, vast, and bizarre love of which we had no inkling; an indispensable love that took the place of our mother's body, now become a ruined dwelling place. Who would invent a new shelter for us? It was this love issuing from the depths of our eyes and our tears that created it, without our knowing, so as to house us, the two of us as closely bound as twins newly paired within the placental membrane. Each holding up the other, hair entwined, so as to stand upright and then proceed with diminished fear.

Little by little, at an interval of several years, words will take hold of us and send us floating away, separately, each on her writer's bark, but linked by that invisible cord.

Silences

She is the first to succumb, but she will recover and survive her beloved by nine years.

In 1976, I published a book devoted to this two-part woman, to her tenacity, to her silences, all carried away in a final coma.

You write, you imagine that you've been unburdened, the way you throw away worn-out suitcases. Not so fast! It's true for a while, time to catch your breath and realize that ghosts, smiling from their frames, are faithfully watching over you. They never stop asking questions and they finally catch us. That's as it should be.

The image of this damaged body, of this broad-shouldered beauty, my mother, a woman who, after her dikes had broken and she'd reached her limits, nevertheless drew herself up to curse a world that had deprived her of so much—the image of this mother exhausted but never giving up stamped itself on my adolescence to the point of nausea.

It wasn't her fault. If she'd been a dwarf with all her limbs amputated, I would have loved her just the same; but how I missed her in her entirety!

You're just like your mother

Again and again I heard this statement from Juliette's mouth. She made it sound like an affectionate, fatalistic reproach; like a warning, too: watch out, don't be too much like her or things will go wrong!

Since she'd joined our family in the '30s, Juliette had had time to get us down pat. She was a compassionate, vivacious onlooker who always knew her place—one in which she knew long before we did that she'd be indispensable.

While our father was away, she became our foster mother, the woman of the household that the rightful mother had to desert to earn our daily bread and make the rounds of lawyers, ministers, and prisons. Juliette brought us up, especially me, the baby, the "daughter she'd seen born."

By remaining loyal to the family of a collaborator (for which she was sometimes cruelly blamed), Juliette, without ever bragging about it, rescued our future from total despair. She knew that we knew it and was proud of that. As her cheerful double, she took over when my mother withdrew into illness and kept us all going, never losing faith in our potential resources. She wasn't mistaken.

She played her role of domestic Cassandra with that mischievous "You're just like your mother," a refrain that told me: "Don't trust people, especially men—look at your father! Don't be a saint like her. You see what that got her." I had been warned.

If later in life I happened to notice certain undeniable features I shared with my mother's character, I don't think I ever thought I had "found myself" in her. I didn't want to, terrified as I was by the weight of accumulated unhappiness that had left her wrecked, dragging her crippled body behind her, poor darling. Full of admiration for her as well during the nine years I was obliged to follow her uneven decline, a "tragedy" in my eyes of which, in spite of everything, she remained the steadfast heroine.

Terror and admiration make poor companions. How can you strike a balance between them?

As the modest translator of the silences of this woman who huddled in her shadowy realm, I made a novel of her life with her as its heroine; but I rejected her role of obedient woman and unquestioning wife, even if I allowed her the extenuating circumstances of belonging to a generation devastated by two wars. The woman I never have disowned, and never will, was the passionately loving she-wolf, the one legacy shining through the ashes that I claim from her: how to be oneself and find the strength to stay that way.

Family members enjoy playing games of resemblance. It lets them—at little cost, they think—explain a number of failings, or failures, or "unfortunate coincidences." It can be a dangerous game unless one decides to go beyond it and look a little deeper into the sources of misfortune.

From the age of fourteen to twenty-six, with no thought of sacrifice, I lived in a state of emergency at my disabled mother's side. I loved her unthinkingly, without any sense of giving up my freedom, even though, once the men in the family were gone, we three females (my "two mothers" and I) found ourselves living in a world apart. With Juliette's support, I thought only of protecting her and keeping her going—I'm not sure how—in a restricted world whose horizon was a black-and-white wall of blurred smiling faces. I thought only of keeping up with her, at her own speed. How far? Did I have the slightest idea?

She knew better than I did. One night at the end of her last silence—a six-week-long coma—she vanished, leaving me like a sleepwalker on the edge of a roof . . . But I was safely out of it. It was my turn to be a mother—my little Émilie was two years old. And then I was able to defend myself: I'd started to write.

I'd had time to tell her about my project and tried to question her. No use. She was frightened at seeing me so determined to reveal our "family secrets" publicly. By tiptoeing out of my life—thank you, *Maman*—she'd given me carte blanche. My words would take the place of hers.

I would later learn that one is not necessarily the slave of resemblances, provided one is willing to identify and abandon them. This requires a certain kind of work—it's the least one can do.

A certain kind of work

For me, it was writing, that very mysterious thing that happens, or doesn't happen, at the precise moment when . . . or perhaps not at all; but never happens "all by itself," a point that bears repeating since many people still believe it does.

A window suddenly opens in the ceiling of the pitch-dark room. If the desire to write unfolds at the same time as its wings, it will—wonder of wonders—find its way out. Beginnings are elating, it's like a first time ever, a mirror that wishes you well—but the desire to write is a little state of grace that must be pampered like a frail, voracious child about to be born. Its first words are babblings that jostle one another to emerge from the dark flood.

Writing for me was a peculiar accident: a process of mourning that at twenty-one I had completed without realizing it. Of mourning for men—father and brother—who betrayed the infinite love with which I could have consoled them, the idiots!

So was it "logical," was I being consistent when another accident, a new spell of mourning for a beloved man, came to interrupt the flow of redeeming words?

While he was alive, I'd never thought of Alain Oulman as a "brother." You don't think about things like that. It's the dead who draw you down to the bottom of the well where stones sleep. When I lost my way, he was the one who had restored my confidence. Losing him sent me back to the process of mourning that I found impossible to recommence, to express again in words. I gave up making any effort; I gave up all desire to write.

Is it any more surprising, any less consistent with the course of things that ten years later I feel abandoned at the moment when the rejected man is obliged to leave, the man who, precisely, told me, "Start writing!" and who called me his "sister"?

The game of resemblances

Last summer we took some friends who were passing through on a tour of the house in Lans. In one nook of the huge granary that Harry uses for an office there are only a couple of photographs on the wall. One romantic oval frames a serious-looking, longhaired young woman. The pale low-necked blouse she's wearing makes it clear that the portrait is fairly recent, despite its intentional sepia tint.

"What a lovely picture!" the woman exclaims. "I've seen that person before. Which one of your daughters is she?"

"It's only me," I say with a laugh. "At thirty-two."

In her embarrassment the woman apologizes profusely.

"Why? I'm delighted to be taken for one of my daughters. They're much more beautiful than I am."

In fact, I could have half-jokingly gone on, that sepia girl (she'd appeared in '74 on the back cover of my first book) isn't half bad after all! It's hard to refer to her as "me." Is she still me? I've been separated from her, too—with regret, obviously.

"The funny thing is," my friend said appeasingly, "your daughters don't look like one another, but one can see something of you in each of them."

Needless to say, that was music to my ears.

The risky game of "you're so like . . ." was of course invented by those inevitable beings called parents, and by the parents of parents stretching beyond them. For reassurance's sake? We're less frightened, aren't we, by the traits we think we recognize through the prism of resemblances, even when these are (let's not kid ourselves) mainly flaws and shortcomings.

We know that most human beings harbor a secret obsession: that of finding themselves or (an even greater gratification) the "best of themselves" in their progeny; even believing

82

they have set right in their progeny the damage done them in their own childhood. We can't escape this will to transfer what we think we've learned; but we've been working on the wrong site, inevitably—there's no right way to do it, or there are too many.

Failure isn't necessarily guaranteed. Poor mothers and fathers, forgetful, aged children, let's soothe our insomnias, let's try and keep our ambitions modest, let's exclude from our vocabulary the sacrosanct "experience" of our forbears and every revolting "certainty." Let's allow our beloved little ones to talk and cry their hearts out. It's their turn! For our pride as responsible parents, what's hardest is to keep quiet at the right moment, while knowing that it may well be (and almost surely is) the worst.

There's nothing we can do for their pain as they seek out their own identities. Let's not aggravate it by driving home the deadly nail on which to hang an oval portrait.

Transference?

More than once I've been told, "You're lucky, you have a good relationship with your daughters, and that's no accident: you got on well with your mother."

No doubt it's true. Among my childhood paraphernalia there weren't only sorrows but a multitude of tiny items passed on to me, trifles that shine like treasures that never burn out, whatever advanced age one reaches. What are these treasures if not childhood itself, broken into pieces that are glued back together with words, colors, beach pebbles, whatever comes to hand . . . On condition that something is restored? Assembling small memories—decals and scraps of all kinds, a medley of jingles . . .

Chocolate bar between two slices of bread—time for your afternoon snack?

Garden, elder tree, sheets shaken out at a window, the house has been sold—and the pink horse-chestnut flowers with it?

Velvety skin, cheek smelling of fruit, maternal breath when she comes home, train at night delight.

Intimate scent of scarves, silk and muslin, snitched in the interval of an absence.

Rings, jacquard knitting, how slow your weariness climbing Mont Valérien.

Chopin waltzes, the Moonlight Sonata and the German language never shall I forget it.

Cinq de Molyneux compact snapping shut (powder mist), and your voice in church, so pure, so other, so beautiful I'm almost ashamed of it.

Smoke rings, Lucky Strike, blue whorls, black coffee . . .

My mother, you've disappeared and yet you walk in silence at the edge of my dreams.

Thus the "good relationship" takes shape, and it keeps moving like a ball passed on from player to player, from mother to daughter. Love and trust—if that sounds old-fashioned, too bad—they constitute our infallible method of transference. It hasn't always been a smooth ride—sometimes the motor overheats or stalls— but it is, I repeat, a question of improvisation, dependent on humor more than on principles; at least I think it is. Love, trust, and every shade of laughter: I stick obstinately to a maternal space in which you can navigate by sight.

I was lucky: the legacy was heavy but the women who did the passing on had a light touch—and, thanks to them, I finally published it for all to see. If you believe that not everything can be told in a book, words still find their own way and, left to themselves, decide where to land.

Love and trust kept flowing between me and the two lovely connections I had for daughters. It happened effortlessly on my side: the child of the '40s must have remembered the air she'd breathed, the atmosphere of pure love that enveloped her in spite of the folly of adults who had escaped disaster.

It wasn't always perfect. We had our rough moments, malignant episodes of adolescence, we fell somewhat out of touch and "conflicts" abounded, very different at the interval of five years between my very dissimilar daughters. Precocious loves and spasms of anxiety. Insomniac dawns waiting for news. And Léonore's punk years! Sound and fury, tortured sulks, Technicolor hairdos. The faces our bourgeois neighbors made! And my own face when I had to plead her case at meetings of the parent-teacher association! Today we giggle helplessly when we talk about those things or see the two of them in snapshots of their dissolute youth.

Now when I look at them, one and the other, I'm dazzled by their beauty, their drollness, their independence, and by the thousand and one unvarnished truths we've inflicted without destroying each other. I wonder how they managed it; since after all what else have I passed on to them besides life, on a first and second of September? They're the ones I'll have to ask, a long time from now. Who they are—what I can see in them today—is their own doing. What I was handing over was something they grasped in the recognition of a moment not to be missed, if they wanted to keep making their way in the great common place into which I'd released them. They've stayed the distance with no help from me. Am I saying they "managed" with what I passed on to them, the thoroughly tangled skein taken from a trunk in my family attic? That is still my version. Up to them to go on asking.

Judging by the complaints I heard, it can't have always been rosy with a mother around who—much too often for their liking—was waving her handkerchief from a train window or the porthole of an airplane. They'll have to write their own version of desertion. For my part, I love them. Wherever I may be and without limit.

If that isn't enough (and haven't we heard all too often that "love isn't enough"?), let them find something else and come tell me about it when I am gray and full of sleep . . .

You ask, what about the father in all this? That is my weak point. It's no use: where I'm concerned, the part fathers play is a thankless one.

Handkerchief at a train window

You're right: I did leave you often. You can't imagine how guilty and torn I felt among my suitcases. It wasn't to get away from you, my lovelies; I would have liked to put you each in a pocket and take you with me, never break up our trio, and go on babbling with you above the clouds.

I admit that more than once, following where love led me, I tore myself away from you and put you in homes where you say our separation used to make you weep. The memory of those homes still haunts you: I swear that you must have transformed them—they were only inoffensive refuges with kindly families. But you were alone there, far from your divided parents, far from your itinerant mother, who left you to the protection of forests and snowbound roads, clinging as she was to the wings of a migrating bird, pursuing her dream of being loved by a man and hearing him tell her so in every hue of the rainbow, and at last believing him.

We remember departures better than returns, don't we? There's more poetry in the lyricism of abandonment than in daily contentment. And we forget the most joyful parts. Later we try to reconstitute the past: that hurts, and we look for help elsewhere.

What do we pass along other than songs that have vanished in the night, scents fluttering in the wake of laughter, blurred images, fragments of a story that even for two beings who have shared them will never be the same? Memories are longings that are rewritten and passed on in the current of words that reinvent them; and so it goes . . .

An unseasonably summery evening in springtime Vermont; a white house on the campus of Bennington College, a typically

American house of painted wood. Nightfall is barely in sight. The babysitter is busy in the kitchen. We're going out to dinner. Harry waits for me at the wheel of our pale metallic-green Buick, the motor running. I'm coming! Just one last kiss for my two hoppingly happy ones, damp and soft after their evening bath. I break away from them and find myself on the porch steps, beyond the screen door that has shut to a squeal of laughter.

Freeze-frame: a mother, breeze in her hair, earrings tinkling, her long billowing dress of Indian cotton printed with roses and mallows that glitter with fragile spangles, fragrance of musk or sandalwood. On the other side of the screen, four little hands as still as startled squirrels, my two household elves, the blonde and the brunette, openmouthed, two pairs of eyes raised in wonder: "*Maman*, you're beautiful!" Did they say it, did I even hear it, astonished to find myself the object of such an outburst of love? The horn honks; I hustle off. There's a rush of laughing that fades away within the white house.

An indelible snapshot of absolute happiness. I've described it to them in every detail. Neither one has the slightest recollection of it.

December 20, 1996

In the visitors' room of a clinic, on a cold afternoon already overtaken by night, Jean-François and I find ourselves sitting alone, hand in hand, in a newly shared complicity of imminent grandparenthood.

"All the same, it's funny, isn't it?" he says.

"You're telling me."

I can barely articulate my words. What seems funny to me is that I'm desperately trying to feel what for the moment I don't feel at all: the emotion of knowing that a few yards away my beloved daughter is giving birth. I'm totally calm. Not nostalgic. Peaceful. The little mother has gotten down to business; she's taken over. It's not up to me anymore.

Hearing the midwife's voice—"Inform the grandmother"—makes me jump and turn around to see if there isn't a grandma nearby, a little lady in black smock and white bun.

Someone else appears at the end of the corridor, and this time we bolt out of our seats. Richard is summoning us from the birthing room threshold, which he isn't allowed to cross. I've never seen him so merry—he's radiating gaiety: "Come on! May I introduce you to my son?"

In his arms is one of Snow White's dwarves in miniature, with a darling bonnet of spotless cotton.

We move toward them. I'm finally "feeling" something: my legs are shaking. Dumbfounded, I say the first thing that comes into my head at the sight of this wise old face with its long nose and knitted brows: "He looks like my father!"

My inner voice immediately starts bawling me out: "No, no, you're not going to start that!" And I run off into the night so that the three men won't see me crying.

His son

Going into the birthing room, he had said he wasn't going to stay for the final stage. At his daughter's birth fourteen years earlier, he "hadn't been able to" and had fled, incapable of facing the spectacle of stains and pains that is childbirth. So he'd played the traditional role—considered reactionary by some—of a father pacing the corridor and smoking one cigarette after the other until the moment when the cry of the child at last rang forth.

Why nowadays do we make such a fuss about the father's presence at the bedside of the woman in labor? I can understand wanting out of a legitimate desire or curiosity to share every one of those first precious moments, but leave the other men be and don't treat them like cripples if they can't endure the sight of the bloodied miracle they've engendered.

During the hours when Jean-François and I were sinking into a lethargy of waiting, I hadn't given another thought as to what Richard might do, or noticed that we hadn't seen him again. Now suddenly he had appeared with his tiny son clasped to him! "It was simple and beautiful," he said, "and I didn't want to leave her."

She who left

They loved each other madly: he'd left everything for her; she used to say, "I love him, I'll never leave him." She lived protected by his strong body, his extravagant words, his unbounded energy.

Being a mother, with a mother's view of things, I was at ease during this time, taking things at face value: my daughter happy with this unpredictable, magnificent man who cared for her, doing her laundry, running the household errands, making the meals, and writing books. Whenever she looked at him her eyes brimmed with love and peace.

It was she who left. Like her own mother? At the same age I'd been when I'd wanted it, she was overcome with longing for a child. He dreaded becoming a father again, "at his age" (nineteen years older than she). I can still hear myself telling him in a tone of maternal reproach, "Listen, you can't marry a twenty-six-year-old woman without supposing that sooner or later she'll want to have a child by you."

But he was frightened—frightened of creating a cartoon couple with a baby and all its accessories. Frightened of creating the typical family scenario that "destroys the couple," he used to say, "and finally destroys love."

And, bang, it happened. Slowly, after a few years, but it happened. Today she says to him, "Don't cry, the past was beautiful."

When one leaves, I remember, one would like the other person to evolve simultaneously and feel like running away too, preferably in the opposite direction, to a change of scenery, to another hemisphere. One would like to place magic bandages on his wounds and over his mouth, so that he'll finally stop talking and not keep reviving with his complaints one's shame at having abandoned him.

He cries out, "No! The past isn't beautiful anymore. It's just a little more past, that's all. Ruins."

Ruins

I'm twenty years old. In a telephone booth in the basement of a café near the Madeleine, I've just learned that my brother, Paul, has died. My sister, at the other end of the line, hesitated to tell me. Her voice betrayed disaster. "Go home. Something's happened." I thought of my mother, so ill. He was ill too, but it must have been unimaginable for me to think of "that" happening. "Paul's dead." Her voice breaking.

Shortly afterward I join Noémi and another college friend, their *cafés-crème* in front of them. I'll never forget their distraught faces looking up at me. I sit down and start crying, with my elbows on the table and my hands hiding my eyes and forehead.

The images that I've kept of this moment, engraved on the inside of my skull, are images of ruins: walls collapsing, the sound of bombs, crumbling houses, and among those houses down which rubble and dust cascade, my own, our own, my family's.

My father died exactly nine months later, stricken with a devastating cancer.

Don't tell me that one always rewrites the same book. I know it.

The summer of the Elder Tree—II

Lans-en-Vercors, July 20, 2000

Richard is visiting for a few days. This summer the boy won't see his parents together except on a train platform or—as in an exchange of hostages—in a parking lot baking in the heat. I haven't forgotten these hurried meetings, so nauseatingly sad.

Let's take a few walks—the three of us. The little boy keeps climbing gamely on his three-and-a-half-year-old legs. Whenever he tires, his father perches him on his shoulders.

I don't take any snapshots—too painful seeing them, the tall man and the tiny boy, without her between them.

July 21

Glorious mountain weather. Not a cloud in the sky. A few late umbels have opened at the top of the elder tree and touch my window.

Another loaded question on the subject of separation: on the phone I'm trying to explain the "state I'm in" to a friend I haven't seen in a long time. Having patiently listened to me:

"But after all, Marie, don't tell me you're surprised?"

I keep silent, pierced to the heart. Can I have been as short-sighted as all that?

July 23. Evening

On the one hand, I understand. Not on the other. I feel jilted. My daughter seems like a stranger. She's elsewhere. Elsewhere. On a cloud with her new love. And I'm jilted. So much for the one hand. But what about the other?

"That's passion," she says in the car she's driving, taking the curves a little too aggressively for my taste. We're coming back up from the Grenoble station where I went with the boy to meet her. I find her transformed—the way she treats her son, the way she drives. "*Maman*, you're not starting to get afraid of riding in a car, are you?"

She's left me behind. Broken free? At last?

That's passion! Speak for yourself. I'm fifty-eight years old and tired. On the back seat with the little boy. Bounced around on the curves. My helpless body (my motherly, my grandmotherly body) out of control, pummeled and gouged by the restless boy now excited to fever pitch by his mother's arrival. That's passion? I try to dig deeper into my rattled memory . . .

Everyone's sleeping under the fragrant summer sky. I walk around the creaky house, noticing the silly toys spread around the edge of the bathtub. Children, grandchildren—that's passion?

I think I'd better go to sleep.

Saturday, July 29

—the anniversary of my American marriage in 1992. (I recall a radiant day and the light it cast on the lawn of the Town Hall in Easthampton, Long Island, New York State. I recall the jovial face of the judge who "sealed our union"; he looked like a chubby priest in his ample black gown—it was a little too short and revealed his incongruous bare feet in their down-at-the-heel Top-Siders.)

Having gone down to the village on an errand, I find myself in the square in front of the church at the instant when its bells start ringing. There then appears a little wedding procession, led by the young bride walking at its head, majestic in her unbelievably beautiful gown: heavy ivory-colored satin with flat pleats that look sculpted, crinoline petticoat, a veil with a long train held in place by a headband. Nothing suggests a grand marriage: just a handful of pleasant-looking people dressed up for a party. Strange, I tell myself, to what extent "the gown" has once again become a fairy-tale dream, an object of exotic splendor.

Why do they all want to be blessed in frills and lace? What are they thinking of?

I recall, early one August, a pink muslin dress as light as a petal, and a slender bride, her hair piled high, coming down the wooden stairs of a house in the Ardèche, her face bright with love . . .

I shall never comprehend this mystery: mystery of the moment when the will to become "a couple" and make a public point of being husband and wife asserts itself, stronger than anything else. A moment when the only thing that matters is to plunge headlong together into the breach opening onto limitless certainty . . . And then the ceremony, the pomp, the sacrament, family and friends all gathered together to celebrate—no questions asked—the mystery of the couple in its sham eternity.

"The incomprehensible" may be what's making the grandmother cry tonight—the woman once in love, the ex-couple-wrecker, now lost face to face with a new failure, at the heart of the summer of the elder tree . . .

Wednesday, August 2

After three wonderful summer days, a magnificent periwinkle-blue sky, here I am at my window half-opened onto greenery steaming with rain.

At La Valette, in the house in the Ardèche, César is doing fine. He's been coughing a bit, but not at night," Richard tells me on the phone, "I'm sure of it because I'm sleeping right beside him." So I imagine Richard and the little boy asleep in the same room. In two days it will be his parents' wedding anniversary . . .

On my table, the last elder flower—picked this morning, a mesh of little starlike blossoms with long pistils and a vivid smell of late summer. The sky is ferrying grayness.

Still in Lans, August 15

The summer flies chaotically by, punctuated by the visits of friends. Évelyne: one of Émilie's childhood buddies, with two young children whom she adores. We talk about "family." A daughter of separated parents, she voices her concern about "not making her children go through that (I don't mean to judge anyone, of course) . . ." (I keep silent and listen to her.) Her obsession, she says, is with seeing that her children have the most wonderful experiences possible, "so they'll have beautiful things to remember."

I break my silence to make fun of her in a kind way and cure her of her illusions. It's a vain hope: the little darlings will always manage to remember other things. This makes her laugh.

August 19, evening

What an absurd business!

Here I am, in the silence of the nighttime countryside. On the second floor, in his mother's old bedroom still full of adolescent odds and ends, a little boy three years and seven months old is sleeping. I've tucked him in and cuddled him, after reading him first one, then a second book his mother and aunt used to adore: *Ten Bears in Summertime* and *Ten Bears in Wintertime*. Alone, just the two of us at the edge of the forest, in this creaky house rustling with vanished childhoods.

Émilie in Paris, alone in her apartment, sorry that she has left her son. Back in Paris to see her lover who has family responsibilities of his own and whom she therefore doesn't see all that often. On the phone she tells me she's in low spirits. "Am I always going to be torn from now on between my child and the man I love?" I'd rather not answer, just let my motherly head think: Of course! I know what it's like to be torn like that, a pain born of a disaster we brought on ourselves. We never get over it, and still we go on living, reconfiguring our life in that new context.

Richard in La Valette with a whole other family. His fine voice over the phone, my consternation when I hear him, my own voice ringing false: "Everything's going fine."

Insidious pangs that consume me: nothing simple anymore, having to live with this breakup. On one side the daughter I love, on the other the man she no longer loves and whom I have a hard time abandoning the father of his child, the little creature asleep upstairs who all by himself incarnates our contradictory emotions.

After an hour's conversation, Émilie is in tears: "And now it's raining! I don't know what I'm doing anymore. What's going to become of me?" The conversation is interrupted by the lover who at last emerges into her night.

That's enough. What about me in all this?

Right now, what most concerns me is this: Harry has set out live traps for the dormice, and I don't want to go look at them. Tomorrow I must absolutely not forget those little prisoners in the attic, before he arrives or they starve to death.

Midnight: "I feel better, don't worry. Thanks for being there. That's what you're good for now, poor darling *Maman*: consoling your daughters!"

Key West, March 22, 2002

Here I am again slamming and banging myself against the classroom wall; the others outside are having fun while I go on moping amid my retinue of migraines, insomnia, and nausea.

A hundred-odd pages. So isn't that almost a book? But it's not the end of the tunnel, I haven't resolved anything, the years have piled up, a compendium of phantom books never finished; and the knot that was choking me hasn't been disentangled.

This morning, in despair at my hopelessness, dragging myself downcast through heat unusually intense even for the tropics, I call Richard. The sound of his voice does me good. I ask him to help me.

"I need a scolding."

"Write for Christ's sake!"

"I don't believe in it anymore."

"You're repeating yourself."

"I swear it's true. I'm up against a wall. Scared. Fed up. Sixty years old! Do you realize? I'm sixty years old. It's ridiculous."

"Dear sister, nobody gives a damn. Break loose! Stop holding back! I'm here for you. Call me whenever you want."

(Ridiculous? Why ridiculous? I'm running away from myself again, with my particular skill at dissipating the little quantity of confidence so laboriously amassed, summoning up my weak, credulous double to make a mockery of it: Look at all these wasted years—you're never going to get there. And superstitious to boot, haunted by the idea that after striving toward a possible conclusion the trap will be sprung before it can be reached.)

Spots of sunlight quivering on the deck are winking at me,

crisscrossed by dozens of lizards racing each other and nimbly avoiding my steps. Some mornings I feel as light as these vibrant little creatures who haven't a care for my age or their own. I forget, close my eyes, and feel my hair, grown long again overnight, caressing my bare back. My waist is slender, my heels have wings for dancing . . .

Fear of what?

In the spring of 1989, I was on the point of completing the final draft of *Le Fils de Marthe*. Alain wanted to publish it in September as one of the novels in the new season. Roger Vrigny used to call me regularly to harass me: "Come on, Marie, just write! You don't have to be a genius to write twenty pages, for heaven's sake!"

Neither Alain nor I wanted this book—already immensely sad—to end "badly." We agreed that Marthe, who had lost her son, would emerge from her mourning and stand on her own feet again. I had an outline; the characters he'd advised me to introduce were waiting for me with outstretched arms; I just had to write.

I was at that point when on a mild April evening, dining peacefully with Harry in our Paris kitchen, I had my first fit. When you don't know what it is, the effect is brutal: you think you're going to die. The English term for this kind of seizure, a "panic attack," is a fitting one. The military vocabulary corresponds to what the body feels: as if it had been assaulted by an unknown enemy. Fear makes it rigid and torments it until, shaken by sobs, it is vanquished.

The young doctors of the public emergency service that I called on several times during the following weeks appeared every time like angels bearing the means of my deliverance. I remember the first of them with tenderness and gratitude. I strode up and down the apartment while waiting for him, with Harry at my heels. (He comforted himself with the thought that "At least it's not a heart attack or a ruptured aneurysm. She wouldn't be running around like a madwoman").

I greeted my good angel from the landing. He was taking the stairs four at a time.

"Hurry! I'm about to die!"

A glance at the dying woman did not alarm him. Once we'd reached the bedroom, he stood facing me, holding me by the wrists, and said with a lovely smile:

"No. You're not going to die. The attack won't last. It's called spasmophilia. Are you going through a rough patch, these days?"

I threw my arms around his neck, letting my fear pour out.

I wished he would stay all night and listen to my life's story: the deaths I've known, the unsuccessful book that I'd restarted and then interrupted. He took his leave, wishing me the best of luck.

"Try to have some fun. Not a barrel of laughs, that story you're writing."

To conclude the spasmophilic interlude—between the attacks themselves and their consequences, I could have filled pages and pages of women's magazines; perhaps picked up a whole new group of readers: women going through menopause and suffering from spasmophilia—I shall simply state that once again the decisive intervention came from my friend Nicole. Tired of seeing me "in this condition," and without asking my opinion, she dragged me to the office of a distinguished psychiatrist who had been recommended to her and whom I immediately adored. I mention this intimate matter only for the pleasure of writing his name: Dr. Verlhomme.[*]

---

[*] Verlhomme: *vers l'homme*, "toward the man."

Not a barrel of laughs

I'm going to describe a rescue by psychoanalysis. There was no rescue and no analysis, only welcome help from "the man" of the fateful name. By interjecting the right questions over several months, he lifted me out of my chasm, and I was able to finish my book.

My "great" discovery during our conversations was realizing that the books we write do not suffice to explain us. That would let us off too easily. And we put so much faith, so much hope in them! We think we've covered a certain amount of ground, and we have. Then we turn around: the landscape has shut down again. Night has fallen. Wrapped in her paper armor, filled with an inexplicable urgency to get somewhere, the frail warrior sets out toward another book, imagining that it will be a different one.

I was still consulting the slender white-haired man, so gentle and discreet in manner, when Alain died, on March 29, 1990. I must have gone back to him a couple of weeks after the event that had just disrupted my life.

My memory is one of bitter disappointment. He failed to react when I poured out my feelings to him. What in my innocence did I expect—consolation? I'd come to announce to him that obviously . . . look what's happened to me now . . . how can you expect me to . . . They're deserting me one after the other. Was he sticking to his prescribed role by not showing the slightest interest in my account of this new bereavement? I was hurt. I didn't understand how he could let me down. Honestly, men! How can you trust them?

Soon after, he informed me that he was retiring, leaving me definitively alone with my sorrows.

I lived through yet another abandonment. Too proud to

ask for help elsewhere. Returning to a silence to which, with every ounce of strength I could muster, I alone had condemned myself. Continuing to record in my notebooks the days of an extremely agreeable life, divided between France and America, as well as the unending complaints of a writer (what a self-centered one!) who wrote nothing more than the beginnings of books that went nowhere. Taking pleasure at the same time in an enthusiasm for making collages (lots more fun than writing)—they were inevitably sort-of autobiographical, narcissistic puzzles, all of them leading me to stumble onto the same realization: "I can't write any more." That was a big help.

Aging body, empty husk

It's unavoidable. The only thing is, you don't believe it. Like death, which you don't believe in either. It had caught me unawares, this travesty of death. My body had mimicked it to frighten me and tell me, Stop, look at yourself—where have you gone?

It lay in wait for me at the edge of a lonely wood, this sordidly named scourge of nature. It suckered me as it had my sisters: a devious affliction that they either don't acknowledge or pretend to disregard. What patronizing looks from young female doctors who don't know what they're talking about.

I didn't know either. The predicted catastrophe was a complete fiction, I'd thought. While it slowly readied itself behind the comely façade of love's passionate combatant, the young mother longing for a child.

As for the aging of the body's cells, which we've already learned about in school, it has to be said that we don't care a hoot about it. But it's working silently away all the while, as it weaves its paralyzing web, waiting for the right moment. Its twin, infertility, keeps similarly quiet, on the watch for its proper niche, an echo from the void where it can nestle.

I wasn't expecting it. "Youth prolonged, the fatal day postponed": in the realm of the synthetic hormone how often have I heard that myth and listened to it for reassurance, pitying the women who expressed their fear of aging more openly than I did. Thank you, science, for winning us an extra ten years, as far looks are concerned.

The monthly flux is so constraining that we tell ourselves: what a joy to one day be free of it! This is a serious mistake.

Awakening to a barren body is more painful than all the cramps and hemorrhages of adolescence.

The pain I'm talking about is discreet. It might well make fun of us: "Surprised you've reached your destination at last? Get rid of your delusions—make your peace with it." But it doesn't say anything. It sneaks into place without glorying in its success.

Between my panic attacks, which each time took a different form, as if really trying to drive me crazy, I did my best to write: nothing but darkness emerged. I was a bruised mass of incomprehension. To find a first glimmer of understanding I was obliged to speak of "my problems" to an old friend, now a doctor, who said to me tentatively, "This story you can't manage to finish, about a dead child—maybe it's no accident that you're writing it now, at a time of your life when sterility—"

I almost hung up on her. "As if I wanted to have children at fifty!"

"Well . . . what about your book?"

The pain I'm talking about isn't a direct, measurable result of inevitable aging. That would make things too simple. It's something distant, more deeply buried, unmentionable. It's a kind of melancholy that dreams of the lost omnipotence it hadn't even realized it possessed. The image of loveliness is blurred and broken. What mirror can we turn toward without crying?

The pain I'm talking about is a dormant pool that wants to be ignored so as to stagnate all the better. It's disturbed only by the protests of a body rebelling against the damage it has endured and crying out its painful truths; expressing them brutally while the mind for its part denies them, ready to stoop to anything that might distract the body from its throes and make it believe: Tough it out, growing old isn't what it used to be, you can get around it—exercise, do yoga, get nutritional advice or cosmetic surgery, and don't forget to take Professor Beaulieu's youth pill . . .

But the pain I'm talking about is tough as nails. It's the

astounded discovery of a lasting deprivation. Where have I gone? I thought I was here, now an unknown woman looks at me and nods her head. She'd like to comfort me, but how can she? The truth is, she's scared to death.

From the depths into which she's plunged, the lovely woman won't retrieve any secret of eternal youth, only nasty aches and the ineluctable defects of her changed body.

Whether she believes this or not won't change anything. Days will pass. She won't fall down like her mother, not yet; but she will, alas, be a different woman, and will get used to it—a different, heavy-hearted woman who looks askance at the sepia-colored portrait of the girl in the attic.

A different woman

This "different woman" who would be me from now on—separated from that other part of my life, stuck on the near side of a divide distancing me from the time when I was young and wrote books—was someone I knew too little when death struck my friend down.

It wasn't his fault (dear man), but his disappearance doused the spark of confidence he had kindled in me and kept burning during our brief friendship.

Alain's death happened "to me" at a moment when I had no strength in reserve. It coincided with my empty-husk frailty and left me face-to-face with this "different woman," a tissue-paper stranger, with no protection, no shield, blaming and cursing this last book that I couldn't even mention, whose title I couldn't pronounce for years to come.

How did I conceive the destructive notion of writing about the death of a child just when infertility was taking hold of me? Where did this story I'd never experienced come from if not the morbid fascination I felt for the silent ordeal endured by my mother, deprived of her two sons? I'd identified myself with her as if by chance in a suicidal attempt at understanding the grief she'd overcome.

The book, however, was born. And now the man who had supported and encouraged me throughout the miraculous delivery, the one who "loved me so that I'd keep writing," left me holding a twice-dead child; left me prey to a grief of which I was sure no one around me would grasp the depth or the extent of the damage it had inflicted upon the future of the inconsolable "different woman" I'd become: so vulnerable, so depleted.

Everything was linked, bound together by one stroke of fate: I won't have other children; I won't write; I'll be a stone.

I who'd lost him

They go away, or stay no longer than for a brief pause in their journey.

I didn't see them leave; I was asleep. Others will tell me white lies.

They go away and never come back.

Always the same ones—brothers, the father, the men of the house. And the house falls down.

I suffer from my brothers' absence. From their betrayal, too: I desperately tried to find them in my first lovers, whom I'd drive away rather than have them give me up.

They leave without saying good-bye, turn their backs, stay away without saying why, and disappear.

I'm sixty-two years old. Almost half the years of my life have been spent in happiness at being loved by a man whom I love and who looks after me. Still, I can never stop rerunning the old movie (it never changes) of loss revived.

Of a man going away, his back toward me: the boy wrapped in his boy scout's cape disappearing one morning under the bombs, or the man in a sheepskin jacket who turns around in his cage when visiting hours are over; the thirty-three-year-old man, the younger brother who walks back down a hospital corridor without knowing it's a last good-bye, or the little man on Rue Auber in his navy-blue overcoat with upturned collar, a delicate bird disappearing into the winter with all the books still left to be written; even the back-country skier who dashes up a forest path in the Vercors wreathed in my irrational fear "that he won't come back."

Absence has been sowing its fear for so long. It's to absence one should say good-bye.

Lost

Without really talking about it, but without hiding it from one another, Richard and I knew what connections with the past we had in common: childhood bereavements, spells of desperate sadness, the violence of walled-up sorrows, and then the redemption of writing that hoisted us back to the present. Even if our way of approaching and exploiting writing is very different, we also knew that we shared the good luck of staying in the world thanks to the words that had reestablished our desire to live.

It was probably no accident in our kinship that both of us, at a few years' interval, had delivered ourselves of a book concerning a father who disseminated failure. Our bond had been cemented by my daughter.

I saw nothing of all this, so I'm filled with anguish when I think back on it. Speaking of "chance" or its absence is, I know, a convenient way of camouflaging an abyss where the inexplicable and the unsaid go to ground. My chronic instability hasn't yet allowed me to explore it.

I see a rope stretched over this abyss. Along it advances the little tightrope walker in her white leotard, sure of herself and her balancing pole, thinking only of the curve of her diminutive foot. She is innocent and serious; she won't let herself be distracted by the dark monsters that writhe and struggle amid their feast of war victims and ruins. The funambulist will make it safe and sound to the far side and there secure her nine years of love.

In wonder I watched and blessed Emilie and Richard, these two unlikely survivors. Meanwhile, in my eyes, Richard (incognito, and without any ado) took on his role as brotherly reconciler of a fragmented family. He was someone who would never leave.

The summerhouses were at last abuzz with family, a family that gathered strength from this preposterous jester. He punctuated its life with endless arguments and wonderful discussions filled with love, laughs, wine, and human feeling, during those starry nights when one thinks one has finally understood.

I believed in this. I used to believe it, egoistically. Was it only a dream that I perpetuated in my daughter—that she at last would find tranquility of heart and mind in an "ideal" first marriage?

No: I must resign myself to it.

It was she who decided to leave, shattering the dream and drowning it in the acid rain of an elder tree. My ravishing, irascible girl who in pigtails one day reenacts the little brunette that I had been, playing hopscotch in the Suresnes garden, and on the next flounces by, a sultry vamp, the small of her back in spangles. The loving mother of a child she had longed for, who would so much like to spare him pain but who knows adamantly what she no longer wants, whether *I* like it or not.

Oh, to tell her at last, "Spread your wings!" and watch her take off. With or without tears. That no longer matters at all.

Summer's end

The trip had been planned a long time ago for late September, 2000. Changing any part of it, because of the feelings of an anxious mother, was inconceivable. On the contrary, I was told that following through would be a welcome diversion.

On the 19th, our friends the writer Ann Beattie and her painter husband Lincoln Perry arrived at the Lyons airport from Rome. They were to spend two nights in Lans, after which we would leave together by car on the morning of the 21st. Destination: Germany. I hadn't set foot there in thirty-five years, except briefly in Berlin in 1991; but Berlin is special.

It was odd that in the end it was a great master of Italian painting, Giambattista Tiepolo, who would make me take the plunge. The goal of our trip was the *Residenz* in Würzburg, in Upper Franconia, a marvel that Harry had been promising me for years.

From 1750 to 1753, at the request of the *Prinzbischof,* Giambattista Tiepolo had created his monumental work: frescoing the huge ceiling that overhangs the no-less immense rise of the stairway and its adjacent spaces. Nothing—not Harry's enthusiastic description of it, nor any reproduction—could give us any idea of the emotions that awaited us.

He had prepared the trip meticulously: each day's distance, each night's hotel. Würzburg was a long way off, and making the journey in two stages would not be excessive. What did I think of going by way of Konstanz on the Bodensee (the German name of Lake Constance)? Was I against the idea? I could see no reason to hold out any longer.

I had never been to Constance nor gone anywhere near its lake, something that seemed absurd to me whenever I thought of the people who so often asked me about it. Their eyes widened at my lack of curiosity. I'd written *Laurels* without bothering to take a closer look, without traveling or in fact trying to make any contact at all with witnesses from that time and place. I had described the island of Mainau, where an essential, tragic moment of my father's adventure took place, by putting my entire trust in the recollections he had studiously recorded in his prison notebooks.

Once that book had been written and published, I spent many years in a state of rancor against Germany. For me it had become an infernal world that it was impossible to approach without fear and loathing. I admit that my rage came late and that my attitude was unfair with regard to the two generations of Germans who, like me, were trying to adjust to an unacceptable past. It had become a fixation. I couldn't stand the sight or sound of them.

As for the German language, almost my mother tongue, since it reached me through my mother and her Saxon forebears, one I'd learned from her and spoken with her before studying it at length in my university years, I was incapable of pronouncing a single word, and soon lost the use of it.

Harry for his part had spent a few months in Germany in the early '60s in order to learn the language at the Goethe Institut in Murnau. Being a conscientious, stubborn man, he speaks it correctly enough.

During our discussions of Germany, a topic that I rejected outright and without nuance, he showed himself to be more open-minded than I, even if his feelings were mixed. He had gone through some very bad moments with the Bavarians and realized, tolerant though he generally was, that if you're revolted by the behavior of certain human beings, you're quickly tempted to identify them with their entire tribe. Nevertheless, he had been dazzled by the architecture of the rococo churches and their exceptional extravagance.

It was raining when we left Lans on the morning of September 21st. In the late afternoon we crossed Lake Constance by ferry from the south to the north bank and spent the night in Meersburg. To the southeast the Alps indented a sky now turning blue. Mainau, on the opposite side, was distantly outlined against the sunset. I refrained from confronting its massive silhouette, feigning the indifference of a hunter who watches his prey on the sly. The lake's wavelets dazzlingly refracted the light. The day had passed so quickly. I was disoriented and expectant.

Having dropped off our luggage at the Villa Bellevue, we had time before nightfall to visit the church at Birnau, the destination of many a pilgrimage, my first rococo church; also the first one that Harry had seen in 1961. My apprenticeship got off to a bad start: I was *not* swept away. Ann and I kept exchanging glances like fidgety little brats. Even if subsequently I was moved (occasionally) by the exuberance of shapes, colors, and gold leaf, and did my best to express this enthusiastically, my husband was never again persuaded of my good faith or able to overcome his disappointment at my attitude in Birnau.

Outside, the air was cool and damp, the soothing amber light was gently fading. In front of the church a gravel esplanade led to a field planted with vines and apple trees that sloped down to the lake. There was no one but us at this ending of the day. Beneath our feet the grass was strewn with an unimaginable profusion of green apples that we set about gathering, tasting, and exchanging, as if playing a game whose rules had been forgotten.

The great dark eye of the lake attracted me vaguely. I hadn't imagined it being so vast. I tried hard to feel "something," telling myself repeatedly, You're at the scene, doesn't that mean anything to you? Well, no. Nothing was forthcoming, not a tear, not a heartbeat, nothing.

Is the only purpose of pilgrimages to prove to us that we needn't have bothered?

"The island of Mainau is a large garden of almost five hundred acres set in the waters of Lake Constance. About a hundred yards distant from the shore, it is connected to the mainland by a foot-bridge wide enough to allow cars to pass. A huge park surrounds the château. Long pathways wind among the rarest species of trees, tall greenhouses in which lush vegetation flourishes, and fragrant rose gardens."

This is what I wrote in *The Laurels* at the beginning of the chapter "Death in February." Rereading these lines, I realize today that, without suspecting it, I was at the time much closer to the reality I discovered in the year 2000 than to what my father saw when he set foot on the island on January 15, 1945, in the midst of a severe cold spell fraught with frost and ice.

That morning of September 22, the turning point between summer and fall, we take the ferry from Meersburg back to Konstanz on the opposite shore. The weather isn't hot. In the distance we make out the peaks of the Alps covered with newly fallen snow. The low, misty sky nevertheless portends, we are told, a fine day.

We glide over the lake, numbed by the wind and the hum of the engines. Little by little, Mainau emerges darkly through slate-blue air. As we draw closer to the island's mass of darker blue, its black contours seeming almost to vibrate against the milky blur of the sky, I can't help thinking of *Die Toteninsel* (The Island of the Dead), Arnold Boecklin's famous painting in the Basel museum. When he painted it in 1880, A. Boecklin (A. B.: same initials as my father!) had initially called it *Ein stiller Platz* (A Peaceful Spot).

The resemblance between the two islands is limited to their being islands, one real, the other imaginary, and to their evoking a journey back toward the dead, each place filled with the mystery of an unhurried approach. Otherwise, the painting has nothing to do with my view of Mainau this morning: it depicts a figure standing in a boat arriving in a crepuscular glow at an island that comprises sheer bright crags bracketing a dark stand of cypresses.

"The island of Mainau—its name so lovely when pronounced in a singsong accent—is a haven of peace, an out-of-the-way excursion where nothing has as yet been demolished by bombs. In the middle of the park, commanding the meadows, the vineyards, the grainfields, and the lake, rises the château. The part that dates from the last century spreads out in numerous luxuriously appointed rooms. Near the château there is a fine inn that in peacetime received tourists. Nowadays a staff of Ukrainians prepares meals there for the lucky exiles of the FPP and for the members of the German diplomatic delegation assigned to Doriot, who occupies one wing of the château.

The island of Mainau is the property of the Swedish crown. For the first time since the beginning of the war it is occupied. By Frenchmen: that is why Sweden has agreed to it."

When we arrived in Konstanz, the sky was clearing. After a mile or two by car along the lakefront, you must stop at a vast parking lot through which stream, all year long, the thousands of tourists come to visit *Die Blumeninsel*, Flower Island, one of the most popular pleasure spots in Germany. Mainau is indeed connected to the shore "by a footbridge," in fact a road along which runs a walkway for the numerous pedestrians who have just gotten out of their cars. We were among them, in the sunlight of this beautiful day twittering with birds, at the edge of the glassy lake where ducks were calmly gliding.

"*Willkommen auf der Insel Mainau!*" announce the brochures and the smiling, pretty face of Sonja Gräfin Bernadotte af Wisborg, whom you can meet on the "Insel Mainau" website and who presides over the destiny of the place. "On Mainau, where palms and orange trees vie in abundance with so many other exotic marvels, you can smell the fragrances of the South. Each season brings a new miracle of nature: tulips in spring as far as the eye can see, roses in summer, dahlias in the fall . . ."

For over three hours we walked around this fabulous garden, wandering down pathways, the rhododendron alley, the hortensia lane, crossing hills of blood-red dahlias, the Italianate rose garden with its arcades and colonnades overlooking the lake, visiting at length the butterfly pavilion (a huge rustling glass-enclosed space), the tropical greenhouses, the smart and spotless baroque château whose ground floor has been turned into a vast showroom. One cannot visit the upper stories, set aside for the apartments of the Bernadotte family that for centuries has managed this exceptional estate.

There is an interesting, lavishly illustrated book devoted to the beauties of the island and the history of the valiant clan that has consecrated its life and wealth to this magnificent place. One learns for example that the present head of the family, Graf Lennart Bernadotte, King Carl XVI Gustav of Sweden's uncle, was born on May 8, 1909 in Stockholm, having among his many titles that of *Erbfürst von Schweden* (Crown Prince of Sweden) and that he was obliged to give it up along with its attendant privileges when in 1932 he married a commoner, his first wife (her name is not mentioned).

One further learns that in 1951, as a reward for his good and faithful services in preserving the precious Flower Island, Graf Lennert, thanks to his aunt, the Grand Duchess Charlotte of Luxemburg, recovered a title, that of *Graf af Wisborg*;

he was thus able to offer it to his second wife, the pretty Sonja we see in an orange suit amid pink dahlias, and transmit it to the five children she bore him. All of which is fine, just, and instructive.

Of course I didn't expect to find in a bright and floral tourist guide any mention of the presence in '44-'45 of Jacques Doriot and his retinue in this four-star refuge. It's odd all the same that between the two dates cited, 1932 and 1951, nineteen years have disappeared from Mainau's history such as it is now commemorated.

In the kingdom of flowers and Swedish princes, neither Hitler nor World War II seem to have existed. The witnesses have died or kept quiet, praying that their descendants will have forgotten everything down to its final flicker, and that the lake's smooth surface will never again be perturbed by the throes of history.

I don't regret having come. I wasn't expecting to find traces any more vivid than those in my memory, nor arrive at any better understanding of why "of all memories, those of childhood are the worst."

Tranquilly, haphazardly, I looked for the two of you along the walkways, I tried to identify the tower where you said you'd worked, the outbuildings where you slept, now become restaurants and souvenir shops (but selling souvenirs that do not evoke you). I looked for you in the shadow of gigantic trees, cedars, sequoias over a hundred years old whose exact age I tried to calculate. Leaning against their bark, eyes raised to their crowns, I imagined your hands touching the same wood and your eyes seeing the branches of the same trees, and this soothed me.

I didn't meet your ghosts. The past is no longer there. The island of the dead is submerged in flowers. In this "peaceful spot" I can at last and without pain let the memory of you rest, and depart.

Constance, September 23, 2000

Fall has come. In three months César will be four years old. Richard is publishing *Ma vie folle*, his ninth novel. He's finished moving. On the phone Émilie tells me that she and the child went to see the apartment where his father is temporarily settled. He inspected everything without a word—the little bedroom reserved for him, the handful of toys, the pots and pans in the kitchen, the doormat, the mailbox.

When they were outside, he asked his mother, "Is he going to come back?"

Surprised, quaking a little, she hesitated five seconds before saying, "No."

He replied, "Okay."

Words spoken on the sidewalk of Rue Rochebrune in Paris this September morning.

MARIE CHAIX was born in Lyons and raised in Paris, and is the author of nine books, including *Silences, or a Woman's life* and *The Laurels of Lake Constance*, both of which are available from Dalkey Archive Press.

HARRY MATHEWS has written over a dozen books, including the novels *Cigarettes, The Journalist,* and *Tlooth.* He divides his time between Paris, Key West, and New York.

SELECTED DALKEY ARCHIVE TITLES

MICHAL AJVAZ, *The Golden Age.*
  The Other City.
PIERRE ALBERT-BIROT, *Grabinoulor.*
YUZ ALESHKOVSKY, *Kangaroo.*
FELIPE ALFAU, *Chromos.*
  Locos.
IVAN ÂNGELO, *The Celebration.*
  The Tower of Glass.
ANTÓNIO LOBO ANTUNES, *Knowledge of Hell.*
  The Splendor of Portugal.
ALAIN ARIAS-MISSON, *Theatre of Incest.*
JOHN ASHBERY AND JAMES SCHUYLER,
  A Nest of Ninnies.
ROBERT ASHLEY, *Perfect Lives.*
GABRIELA AVIGUR-ROTEM, *Heatwave
  and Crazy Birds.*
DJUNA BARNES, *Ladies Almanack.*
  Ryder.
JOHN BARTH, *LETTERS.*
  Sabbatical.
DONALD BARTHELME, *The King.*
  Paradise.
SVETISLAV BASARA, *Chinese Letter.*
MIQUEL BAUÇÀ, *The Siege in the Room.*
RENÉ BELLETTO, *Dying.*
MAREK BIEŃCZYK, *Transparency.*
ANDREI BITOV, *Pushkin House.*
ANDREJ BLATNIK, *You Do Understand.*
LOUIS PAUL BOON, *Chapel Road.*
  My Little War.
  Summer in Termuren.
ROGER BOYLAN, *Killoyle.*
IGNÁCIO DE LOYOLA BRANDÃO,
  Anonymous Celebrity.
  Zero.
BONNIE BREMSER, *Troia: Mexican Memoirs.*
CHRISTINE BROOKE-ROSE, *Amalgamemnon.*
BRIGID BROPHY, *In Transit.*
GERALD L. BRUNS, *Modern Poetry and
  the Idea of Language.*
GABRIELLE BURTON, *Heartbreak Hotel.*
MICHEL BUTOR, *Degrees.*
  Mobile.
G. CABRERA INFANTE, *Infante's Inferno.*
  Three Trapped Tigers.
JULIETA CAMPOS,
  The Fear of Losing Eurydice.
ANNE CARSON, *Eros the Bittersweet.*
ORLY CASTEL-BLOOM, *Dolly City.*
LOUIS-FERDINAND CÉLINE, *Castle to Castle.*
  Conversations with Professor Y.
  London Bridge.
  Normance.
  North.
  Rigadoon.
MARIE CHAIX, *The Laurels of Lake Constance.*
HUGO CHARTERIS, *The Tide Is Right.*
ERIC CHEVILLARD, *Demolishing Nisard.*
MARC CHOLODENKO, *Mordechai Schamz.*
JOSHUA COHEN, *Witz.*
EMILY HOLMES COLEMAN, *The Shutter
  of Snow.*
ROBERT COOVER, *A Night at the Movies.*
STANLEY CRAWFORD, *Log of the S.S. The
  Mrs Unguentine.*
  Some Instructions to My Wife.
RENÉ CREVEL, *Putting My Foot in It.*
RALPH CUSACK, *Cadenza.*
NICHOLAS DELBANCO, *The Count of Concord.*
  Sherbrookes.
NIGEL DENNIS, *Cards of Identity.*

PETER DIMOCK, *A Short Rhetoric for
  Leaving the Family.*
ARIEL DORFMAN, *Konfidenz.*
COLEMAN DOWELL,
  Island People.
  Too Much Flesh and Jabez.
ARKADII DRAGOMOSHCHENKO, *Dust.*
RIKKI DUCORNET, *The Complete
  Butcher's Tales.*
  The Fountains of Neptune.
  The Jade Cabinet.
  Phosphor in Dreamland.
WILLIAM EASTLAKE, *The Bamboo Bed.*
  Castle Keep.
  Lyric of the Circle Heart.
JEAN ECHENOZ, *Chopin's Move.*
STANLEY ELKIN, *A Bad Man.*
  *Criers and Kibitzers, Kibitzers
  and Criers.*
  The Dick Gibson Show.
  The Franchiser.
  The Living End.
  Mrs. Ted Bliss.
FRANÇOIS EMMANUEL, *Invitation to a
  Voyage.*
SALVADOR ESPRIU, *Ariadne in the
  Grotesque Labyrinth.*
LESLIE A. FIEDLER, *Love and Death in
  the American Novel.*
JUAN FILLOY, *Op Oloop.*
ANDY FITCH, *Pop Poetics.*
GUSTAVE FLAUBERT, *Bouvard and Pécuchet.*
KASS FLEISHER, *Talking out of School.*
FORD MADOX FORD,
  The March of Literature.
JON FOSSE, *Aliss at the Fire.*
  Melancholy.
MAX FRISCH, *I'm Not Stiller.*
  Man in the Holocene.
CARLOS FUENTES, *Christopher Unborn.*
  Distant Relations.
  Terra Nostra.
  Where the Air Is Clear.
TAKEHIKO FUKUNAGA, *Flowers of Grass.*
WILLIAM GADDIS, *J R.*
  The Recognitions.
JANICE GALLOWAY, *Foreign Parts.*
  The Trick Is to Keep Breathing.
WILLIAM H. GASS, *Cartesian Sonata
  and Other Novellas.*
  Finding a Form.
  A Temple of Texts.
  The Tunnel.
  Willie Masters' Lonesome Wife.
GÉRARD GAVARRY, *Hoppla! 1 2 3.*
ETIENNE GILSON,
  The Arts of the Beautiful.
  Forms and Substances in the Arts.
C. S. GISCOMBE, *Giscome Road.*
  Here.
DOUGLAS GLOVER, *Bad News of the Heart.*
WITOLD GOMBROWICZ,
  A Kind of Testament.
PAULO EMÍLIO SALES GOMES, *P's Three
  Women.*
GEORGI GOSPODINOV, *Natural Novel.*
JUAN GOYTISOLO, *Count Julian.*
  Juan the Landless.
  Makbara.
  Marks of Identity.

SELECTED DALKEY ARCHIVE TITLES

HENRY GREEN, *Back.*
Blindness.
Concluding.
Doting.
Nothing.
JACK GREEN, *Fire the Bastards!*
JIŘÍ GRUŠA, *The Questionnaire.*
MELA HARTWIG, *Am I a Redundant
  Human Being?*
JOHN HAWKES, *The Passion Artist.*
Whistlejacket.
ELIZABETH HEIGHWAY, ED., *Contemporary
  Georgian Fiction.*
ALEKSANDAR HEMON, ED.,
Best European Fiction.
AIDAN HIGGINS, *Balcony of Europe.*
Blind Man's Bluff
Bornholm Night-Ferry.
Flotsam and Jetsam.
Langrishe, Go Down.
Scenes from a Receding Past.
KEIZO HINO, *Isle of Dreams.*
KAZUSHI HOSAKA, *Plainsong.*
ALDOUS HUXLEY, *Antic Hay.*
Crome Yellow.
Point Counter Point.
Those Barren Leaves.
Time Must Have a Stop.
NAOYUKI II, *The Shadow of a Blue Cat.*
GERT JONKE, *The Distant Sound.*
Geometric Regional Novel.
Homage to Czerny.
The System of Vienna.
JACQUES JOUET, *Mountain R.*
Savage.
Upstaged.
MIEKO KANAI, *The Word Book.*
YORAM KANIUK, *Life on Sandpaper.*
HUGH KENNER, *Flaubert.*
Joyce and Beckett: The Stoic Comedians.
Joyce's Voices.
DANILO KIŠ, *The Attic.*
Garden, Ashes.
The Lute and the Scars
Psalm 44.
A Tomb for Boris Davidovich.
ANITA KONKKA, *A Fool's Paradise.*
GEORGE KONRÁD, *The City Builder.*
TADEUSZ KONWICKI, *A Minor Apocalypse.*
The Polish Complex.
MENIS KOUMANDAREAS, *Koula.*
ELAINE KRAF, *The Princess of 72nd Street.*
JIM KRUSOE, *Iceland.*
AYŞE KULIN, *Farewell: A Mansion in
  Occupied Istanbul.*
EMILIO LASCANO TEGUI, *On Elegance
  While Sleeping.*
ERIC LAURRENT, *Do Not Touch.*
VIOLETTE LEDUC, *La Bâtarde.*
EDOUARD LEVÉ, *Autoportrait.*
Suicide.
MARIO LEVI, *Istanbul Was a Fairy Tale.*
DEBORAH LEVY, *Billy and Girl.*
JOSÉ LEZAMA LIMA, *Paradiso.*
ROSA LIKSOM, *Dark Paradise.*
OSMAN LINS, *Avalovara.*
The Queen of the Prisons of Greece.
ALF MAC LOCHLAINN,
The Corpus in the Library.
Out of Focus.
RON LOEWINSOHN, *Magnetic Field(s).*
MINA LOY, *Stories and Essays of Mina Loy.*

D. KEITH MANO, *Take Five.*
MICHELINE AHARONIAN MARCOM,
The Mirror in the Well.
BEN MARCUS,
The Age of Wire and String.
WALLACE MARKFIELD,
Teitlebaum's Window.
To an Early Grave.
DAVID MARKSON, *Reader's Block.*
Wittgenstein's Mistress.
CAROLE MASO, *AVA.*
LADISLAV MATEJKA AND KRYSTYNA
  POMORSKA, EDS.,
*Readings in Russian Poetics:
  Formalist and Structuralist Views.*
HARRY MATHEWS, *Cigarettes.*
The Conversions.
*The Human Country: New and
  Collected Stories.*
The Journalist.
My Life in CIA.
Singular Pleasures.
*The Sinking of the Odradek
  Stadium.*
Tlooth.
JOSEPH MCELROY,
Night Soul and Other Stories.
ABDELWAHAB MEDDEB, *Talismano.*
GERHARD MEIER, *Isle of the Dead.*
HERMAN MELVILLE, *The Confidence-Man.*
AMANDA MICHALOPOULOU, *I'd Like.*
STEVEN MILLHAUSER, *The Barnum Museum.*
In the Penny Arcade.
RALPH J. MILLS, JR., *Essays on Poetry.*
MOMUS, *The Book of Jokes.*
CHRISTINE MONTALBETTI, *The Origin of Man.*
Western.
OLIVE MOORE, *Spleen.*
NICHOLAS MOSLEY, *Accident.*
Assassins.
Catastrophe Practice.
Experience and Religion.
A Garden of Trees.
Hopeful Monsters.
Imago Bird.
Impossible Object.
Inventing God.
Judith.
Look at the Dark.
Natalie Natalia.
Serpent.
Time at War.
WARREN MOTTE,
*Fables of the Novel: French Fiction
  since 1990.*
*Fiction Now: The French Novel in
  the 21st Century.*
*Oulipo: A Primer of Potential
  Literature.*
GERALD MURNANE, *Barley Patch.*
Inland.
YVES NAVARRE, *Our Share of Time.*
Sweet Tooth.
DOROTHY NELSON, *In Night's City.*
Tar and Feathers.
ESHKOL NEVO, *Homesick.*
WILFRIDO D. NOLLEDO, *But for the Lovers.*
FLANN O'BRIEN, *At Swim-Two-Birds.*
The Best of Myles.
The Dalkey Archive.
The Hard Life.
The Poor Mouth.

The Third Policeman.
CLAUDE OLLIER, *The Mise-en-Scène.*
Wert and the Life Without End.
GIOVANNI ORELLI, *Walaschek's Dream.*
PATRIK OUŘEDNÍK, *Europeana.*
The Opportune Moment, 1855.
BORIS PAHOR, *Necropolis.*
FERNANDO DEL PASO, *News from the Empire.*
Palinuro of Mexico.
ROBERT PINGET, *The Inquisitory.*
Mahu or The Material.
Trio.
MANUEL PUIG, *Betrayed by Rita Hayworth.*
The Buenos Aires Affair.
Heartbreak Tango.
RAYMOND QUENEAU, *The Last Days.*
Odile.
Pierrot Mon Ami.
Saint Glinglin.
ANN QUIN, *Berg.*
Passages.
Three.
Tripticks.
ISHMAEL REED, *The Free-Lance Pallbearers.*
The Last Days of Louisiana Red.
Ishmael Reed: The Plays.
Juice!
Reckless Eyeballing.
The Terrible Threes.
The Terrible Twos.
Yellow Back Radio Broke-Down.
JASIA REICHARDT, *15 Journeys Warsaw to London.*
NOËLLE REVAZ, *With the Animals.*
JOÃO UBALDO RIBEIRO, *House of the Fortunate Buddhas.*
JEAN RICARDOU, *Place Names.*
RAINER MARIA RILKE, *The Notebooks of Malte Laurids Brigge.*
JULIÁN RÍOS, *The House of Ulysses.*
Larva: A Midsummer Night's Babel.
Poundemonium.
Procession of Shadows.
AUGUSTO ROA BASTOS, *I the Supreme.*
DANIËL ROBBERECHTS, *Arriving in Avignon.*
JEAN ROLIN, *The Explosion of the Radiator Hose.*
OLIVIER ROLIN, *Hotel Crystal.*
ALIX CLEO ROUBAUD, *Alix's Journal.*
JACQUES ROUBAUD, *The Form of a City Changes Faster, Alas, Than the Human Heart.*
The Great Fire of London.
Hortense in Exile.
Hortense Is Abducted.
The Loop.
Mathematics:
The Plurality of Worlds of Lewis.
The Princess Hoppy.
Some Thing Black.
RAYMOND ROUSSEL, *Impressions of Africa.*
VEDRANA RUDAN, *Night.*
STIG SÆTERBAKKEN, *Siamese.*
Self Control.
LYDIE SALVAYRE, *The Company of Ghosts.*
The Lecture.
The Power of Flies.
LUIS RAFAEL SÁNCHEZ,
Macho Camacho's Beat.
SEVERO SARDUY, *Cobra & Maitreya.*

NATHALIE SARRAUTE,
Do You Hear Them?
Martereau.
The Planetarium.
ARNO SCHMIDT, *Collected Novellas.*
Collected Stories.
Nobodaddy's Children.
Two Novels.
ASAF SCHURR, *Motti.*
GAIL SCOTT, *My Paris.*
DAMION SEARLS, *What We Were Doing and Where We Were Going.*
JUNE AKERS SEESE,
Is This What Other Women Feel Too?
What Waiting Really Means.
BERNARD SHARE, *Inish.*
Transit.
VIKTOR SHKLOVSKY, *Bowstring.*
Knight's Move.
A Sentimental Journey: Memoirs 1917–1922.
Energy of Delusion: A Book on Plot.
Literature and Cinematography.
Theory of Prose.
Third Factory.
Zoo, or Letters Not about Love.
PIERRE SINIAC, *The Collaborators.*
KJERSTI A. SKOMSVOLD, *The Faster I Walk, the Smaller I Am.*
JOSEF ŠKVORECKÝ, *The Engineer of Human Souls.*
GILBERT SORRENTINO,
Aberration of Starlight.
Blue Pastoral.
Crystal Vision.
Imaginative Qualities of Actual Things.
Mulligan Stew.
Pack of Lies.
Red the Fiend.
The Sky Changes.
Something Said.
Splendide-Hôtel.
Steelwork.
Under the Shadow.
W. M. SPACKMAN, *The Complete Fiction.*
ANDRZEJ STASIUK, *Dukla.*
Fado.
GERTRUDE STEIN, *The Making of Americans.*
A Novel of Thank You.
LARS SVENDSEN, *A Philosophy of Evil.*
PIOTR SZEWC, *Annihilation.*
GONÇALO M. TAVARES, *Jerusalem.*
Joseph Walser's Machine.
Learning to Pray in the Age of Technique.
LUCIAN DAN TEODOROVICI,
Our Circus Presents . . .
NIKANOR TERATOLOGEN, *Assisted Living.*
STEFAN THEMERSON, *Hobson's Island.*
The Mystery of the Sardine.
Tom Harris.
TAEKO TOMIOKA, *Building Waves.*
JOHN TOOMEY, *Sleepwalker.*
JEAN-PHILIPPE TOUSSAINT, *The Bathroom.*
Camera.
Monsieur.
Reticence.
Running Away.
Self-Portrait Abroad.
Television.
The Truth about Marie.

SELECTED DALKEY ARCHIVE TITLES

DUMITRU TSEPENEAG, *Hotel Europa.*
  The Necessary Marriage.
  Pigeon Post.
  Vain Art of the Fugue.
ESTHER TUSQUETS, *Stranded.*
DUBRAVKA UGRESIC, *Lend Me Your Character.*
  Thank You for Not Reading.
TOR ULVEN, *Replacement.*
MATI UNT, *Brecht at Night.*
  Diary of a Blood Donor.
  Things in the Night.
ÁLVARO URIBE AND OLIVIA SEARS, EDS.,
  Best of Contemporary Mexican Fiction.
ELOY URROZ, *Friction.*
  The Obstacles.
LUISA VALENZUELA, *Dark Desires and
  the Others.*
  He Who Searches.
PAUL VERHAEGHEN, *Omega Minor.*
AGLAJA VETERANYI, *Why the Child Is
  Cooking in the Polenta.*
BORIS VIAN, *Heartsnatcher.*
LLORENÇ VILLALONGA, *The Dolls' Room.*
TOOMAS VINT, *An Unending Landscape.*
ORNELA VORPSI, *The Country Where No
  One Ever Dies.*
AUSTRYN WAINHOUSE, *Hedyphagetica.*
CURTIS WHITE, *America's Magic Mountain.*
  The Idea of Home.
  Memories of My Father Watching TV.
  Requiem.

DIANE WILLIAMS, *Excitability:
  Selected Stories.*
  Romancer Erector.
DOUGLAS WOOLF, *Wall to Wall.*
  Ya! & John-Juan.
JAY WRIGHT, *Polynomials and Pollen.*
  *The Presentable Art of Reading
  Absence.*
PHILIP WYLIE, *Generation of Vipers.*
MARGUERITE YOUNG, *Angel in the Forest.*
  Miss MacIntosh, My Darling.
REYOUNG, *Unbabbling.*
VLADO ŽABOT, *The Succubus.*
ZORAN ŽIVKOVIĆ, *Hidden Camera.*
LOUIS ZUKOFSKY, *Collected Fiction.*
VITOMIL ZUPAN, *Minuet for Guitar.*
SCOTT ZWIREN, *God Head.*

FOR A FULL LIST OF PUBLICATIONS, VISIT:
www.dalkeyarchive.com